A
Harlequin
Romance

WELCOME

TO THE WONDERFUL WORLD

of Harlequin Romances!

Interesting, informative and entertaining,
each Harlequin Romance portrays an appealing
love story. Harlequin Romances take you
to faraway places — places with real people
facing real love situations — and
you become part of their story.

As publishers of Harlequin Romances, we're extremely
proud of our books (we've been publishing
them since 1954). We're proud also that Harlequin
Romances are North America's most-read
paperback romances.

Eight new titles are released every month and are
sold at nearly all book-selling stores across
Canada and the United States.

A free catalogue listing all available Harlequin Romances
can be yours by writing to the

HARLEQUIN READER SERVICE,
M.P.O. Box 707, Niagara Falls, N.Y. 14302.
Canadian address: Stratford, Ontario, Canada.

or use order coupon at back of book.

We sincerely hope you enjoy reading
this Harlequin Romance.

Yours truly,

THE PUBLISHERS
    Harlequin Romances

SHADOW OF THE PAST

by

MONICA DOUGLAS

HARLEQUIN BOOKS

TORONTO
WINNIPEG

Original hard cover edition published in 1973
by Mills & Boon Limited

© Monica Douglas 1973

SBN 373-01706-5

Harlequin edition published August, 1973

1706   Printed in Canada

CHAPTER I

It had been raining when Sara Blake stepped off the plane from America, and it was still raining steadily when the taxi drew up at the block of flats which was her final destination.

She stood for a moment, looking at the dreary prospect, and her already low spirits sank even further. It was exactly, she thought, as if the skies had decided to form a fitting background to her sad and sudden homecoming.

She turned as the commissionaire came through the ornate doors and greeted her questioningly.

'I want Mrs Blake's flat, please,' she said.

'That's the penthouse floor. This way, madam.'

He picked up her case and she followed him through the luxurious entrance hall into the lift, which swept them quickly upward, then along a thickly carpeted corridor to a door half way along it.

He rang the bell and as they waited for it to be answered said chattily,

'Mrs Blake's in, I know. She doesn't go out much, not since Mr Blake's death. That was a very terrible thing, wasn't it, madam?'

'Yes,' Sara answered briefly, and was relieved when at that moment the door opened, knowing that she could not bear to talk about her half-brother's tragic death, so recently heard about, with a stranger.

'Sara! At last! I was beginning to think you'd never come.'

Valerie Blake flung her arms around her sister-in-law, taking no notice of the commissionaire who still stood, holding Sara's case, watching them with interest.

Sara kissed her and loosened the clinging arms.

'I came as soon as I could, Val.' She turned to the commissionaire. 'If you'll bring the case in, please—'

She waited until he had put it down in the square hall, then tipped him and said firmly,

'Thank you. That will be all.'

'Thank you, madam,' he answered, and made a dignified exit.

'I wish I was as good as you are at getting rid of all the nosey-parkers,' Valerie sighed.

Sara took off her coat and flung it over the nearest chair, shaking back her thick honey-gold hair.

'Has it been very bad, Val?'

'Yes, simply terrible. I don't know how I've managed. Why didn't you come before, Sara? You must have known how much I needed you.'

'I'm sorry, dear. Johnnie and I were travelling around the country and your cables were delivered to my apartment. I didn't get them until I arrived home. Johnnie got me on the first available plane.

What happened, Val?'

Valerie opened a door at the end of the hall.

'Come in here and I'll tell you all about it. I've made some sandwiches. Do you want coffee or tea?'

'Tea, please. Gallons of it. I'm so thirsty.'

Sara followed her into the ultra-modern kitchen, one part of her mind noting the expensive fittings while the other was concentrated on what her sister-in-law was telling her, between nervous puffs at the cigarette she had lit.

'Was he killed—instantly, Val?'

'Yes. I couldn't believe it at first. David was always going to Paris. He was used to the traffic there. It didn't seem possible that he could have been killed.'

'No.'

'It was awful, Sara. I thought I'd go mad in those first few days. I don't know what I'd have done without Terry. He saw to everything.'

'The funeral?'

'Yes. He went over to Paris and arranged it all. David was buried over there. I thought it best,' she added defensively.

'You were probably right, dear,' Sara said, but in her heart she wished passionately that circumstances had not conspired so that she had not been there to follow her beloved half-brother on his last journey. 'I'm glad Terry was still at Blake's to help you.'

Valerie looked at her in surprise.

'Why shouldn't he be?'

'Oh, no reason.'

Sara's reply was casual because she did not want to put into words her own conviction that Terry White was ambitious and thrusting. She would never have been surprised to hear that he had gone to work for another company where he might have more opportunity for promotion than he had ever had at Blake's Store.

But apparently she had been mistaken, and she was thankful now that he, with his valuable knowledge of the family firm, should be still there to help them.

'He's taken charge at the store, you know.'

'Has he? How's the business going, Val?'

'I've no idea.' Val's voice was offhand and uninterested. 'You know I don't know anything about it. David never discussed it with me. Even after he sold the house and used the money on the store—*my* money, Sara, because my father bought the house for me—he didn't tell me what he was doing.'

'He didn't tell me much either,' Sara said, remembering guiltily that she had been too engrossed in her own job to have any time to spare for Blake's. 'I only heard from him when he wanted me to back him as the only other shareholder.'

'Terry says I'll get David's shares now because I'm his wife. He says I'll be in control, so he's been telling me all about everything, but I don't understand half he says. It all sounds so depressing, too.'

'Terry told you that? But—'

She stopped, and after a moment Val asked enquiringly,

'But what?'

'Oh, nothing really. What's so depressing about everything?'

'Oh, I don't know. He was saying something about the business being deep in debt to a man called Maxwell. At least I think that's the name.'

'In debt? That's not possible. And who's Maxwell?'

Valerie shrugged.

'I've no idea. Anyway, I may have the name wrong. You know I'm no good at business things, Sara.'

'Never mind, love. I'm here now and I'll see to everything for you.'

'You're going to stay, then?' Val asked eagerly.

'For a week or two, anyway.'

'Is that all? Oh, Sara, you can't go away so soon and leave me here all alone. I'll never be able to stand it—'

'But we're so busy, Johnnie and I. Things are pretty hectic in our particular world of finance—'

'Oh, he can spare you, I'm sure. You can't be all that necessary.'

Sara smiled.

'Johnnie thinks I am.'

'Does he?' Val looked at her eagerly, her volatile mind immediately diverted by the implication she thought she could read in Sara's answer. 'Is he in love with you, Sara? Are you going to be married?'

'Here, don't go so fast!' Then as she saw the disappointment in Val's expressive face, she added, 'He says he is, and I've never yet met anyone I like better than him.'

'I'm so glad, Sara. I hope things turn out better for you than they have for me.' Val's china blue eyes filled with ready tears. 'You don't know what it's like to be left alone so suddenly.'

Sara took her hand in both of hers.

'Don't cry, Val. And remember, you're not really alone. You've still got Jamie.'

'But he's away at school all the time.'

'Hasn't he been home at all?'

'No. The Headmaster said it'd be better if he didn't come.'

'He was probably quite right.'

'He was not! My son should have been here with me. Oh, Sara, what's going to become of us both if there's really no money?'

'Who said there's no money?'

' Terry.'

' You must have misunderstood him, Val. Blake's has always been a profitable business, and the last accounts I saw looked very healthy indeed.'

' Did they really, Sara?'

' Yes. Now you're to stop worrying. I'll go and see Terry tomorrow and get everything cleared up.'

Val smiled at her gratefully.

' I'm so glad you've come home, Sara. Now everything will be all right, I know it will.'

It was late when they went to bed that night and Sara did not wake as early as she had planned the next morning. It was afternoon when she left the flat to go to the store, but she was not worried. In spite of what Valerie had told her, she was sure there was very little to worry about.

Because she had really seen the flat that morning and had been astonished by its luxuriousness. The rich carpeting, curtains and furniture must, she was sure, have cost many thousands of pounds, and if David had been able to continue to live there, there could be very little wrong with the family business.

She felt a nostalgic stirring of memory as she walked along the street where Blake's Store had been since it was first opened by her father.

It had been one small draper's shop then, but as time went on he had bought the shops on each side and expanded into them. But it had remained a conservative and rather old-fashioned drapery store, and while Sara had sympathised with her half-brother's desire to modernise it, she had felt rather sad because in the process it was bound to change.

Though even so, she was not prepared for the drastic changes which had taken place and had walked past the store before she realised she had done so.

She went slowly back again, seeing the magnificent new windows, the costly window dressing and the imposing entrance which had taken the place of the double doors that had been an innovation in the last years of her father's life, and knew the first stirrings of doubt.

For nothing David had told her in his infrequent letters had prepared her for the very extensive alterations which had been made. She could hardly recognise it as the same place.

People passed and re-passed her, but she did not see them, though the business side of her brain, so well trained in America by Johnnie, noted that the site was still a busy one, as her father had always said it was.

She shook her head and went into the store, the glass doors opening automatically and closing behind her as she stepped on and off the mat laid before them. The store was brilliantly lighted and very busy, but it was all completely strange to her and it was a while before she knew in which direction to go.

Three years earlier, when she had left home to go to America, a dark staircase had led to the upper floor where the workshops and her father's office had been.

Now, at the rear of the store, an escalator moved on its endless way upwards, and she stepped on to it, to be whisked into an opulent, perfumed foyer with a white and gold table set on a rich deep blue carpet whose colour was picked up in the velvet upholstery of a number of fragile chairs, the whole reflected again and again in the mirrors lining the walls.

There was no one seated at the table and she hesitated, wondering where she could find Terry, and as she did so she saw with relief a woman walking towards her along a side passageway.

'Excuse me, could you tell me—' Sara began, then started forward, her dark eyes lighting up in a smile. 'Mollie! Is it really you? Am I pleased to see you!'

The woman stared at her in astonishment.

'Why, Sara! I didn't know you'd come home.'

'I only arrived yesterday. How are things going here?'

Mollie hesitated.

'All right, I suppose,' she said at last. 'Not that I know very much about it. We certainly

13

seem busy enough, but there've been a lot of changes, as you can see.'

'Yes, indeed. It looks like something at Palm Beach. It must have cost thousands, Mollie.'

'I suppose so. It seems to be paying off all right.'

Sara looked at her, puzzled by her tone.

'Don't you know? I'd have thought in your job—'

'I'm not first sales any more, Sara, so I'm out of touch. Célèste is in charge now. Mr White brought her over from France a couple of years ago. I'm in the sewing room, a kind of glorified storekeeper, really.'

Mollie's voice was harsh with the bitterness of failure, and Sara put her hand gently on her arm in an attempt to comfort her.

'That's a very important job, Mollie. You know what Dad always said—the store couldn't function without an efficient sewing room and storekeeper. That's true, isn't it?'

'I suppose so. I'm lucky to be here at all. Most of the old hands have gone now and those of us who are left—we don't know from day to day what's going to happen.'

She broke off, and Sara realised for the first time that this woman who had been with her father for so many years was no longer young. And she was afraid, deeply afraid that she might lose her job and, perhaps, find it difficult or even impossible to get another one.

'Don't worry, Mollie. I'm back now and I'll see you're all right,' Sara said impulsively.

Mollie smiled.

'Thank you, though I don't suppose you'll want to stay here. You'll have grown away from us all, and I wouldn't blame you for that. Eh, but things have changed since your father died.'

'He would have been the first to say we ought to move with the times,' Sara reminded her.

'Yes, but not run past them. They do say that things are pretty bad. That Brent Maxwell is the real owner—'

'Brent Maxwell.' Sara echoed the name, remembering Val's mention of it the previous day. 'Who is he, Mollie? And how can he be the owner? We're the owners, Mrs David and me.'

Mollie flushed uncomfortably.

'I'm only repeating rumours and gossip, Sara, something I've never done before. But there's a lot of unrest and conjecture in the store. What am I thinking about?' she added, obviously changing the subject. 'Going on like this and never saying a word about your loss!'

'It's all right, Mollie. It's—it's difficult to believe, but—'

'Those Paris drivers! Everyone says they're a menace! Though Mr David had been over there so often you'd have thought he'd be well used to them, wouldn't you? And his lovely car he was so proud of, all smashed up, too. I suppose it was a case of familiarity breeding contempt,' she finished, with a sigh.

'I expect so. I'd better go and find Terry. Is he still in the same office?'

'No. He moved into Mr David's after— The one your father used to have. That way, Sara.'

'I see,' Sara said slowly. 'Thanks, Mollie. I'm glad you were the first person I met. It's made me feel less—strange.'

CHAPTER II

Sara watched her until she was out of sight, then went slowly along the passage towards the office which had been her father's, then David's, and which had now been appropriated by Terry, her feet making no sound on the thick carpet.

She had accepted what Mollie had said without showing any reaction, as if she had thought it a perfectly natural thing for Terry to have done. But beneath her calm exterior she was aware of a resentment out of all proportion to the offence.

She stopped outside the white door, remembering how often she had turned the handle and run into her father's office when she was a child. Only then the paintwork had been dark and chipped, giving no indication of the fairyland of colour waiting for her inside.

It had been like walking into a magic cave in those days, filled as the room always was with patterns and bolts of material in all the colours of the rainbow, piled on every available surface, filling the office with gaiety and brilliance.

Perhaps this memory was responsible for the nervous hesitation which made her reluctant to open the door and go inside. Then she squared her shoulders resolutely. Why should she be afraid? This was not a 'Pandora's box' which she was about to open. She was merely going to see and talk to a man whom she had known for years, who, when she was a schoolgirl, had been a kind of hero to her in those impressionable years before she had gone to America.

She pressed down the ornate gilt handle quickly and went in without giving herself any more time to think, and the two people standing behind the huge desk in the meticulously tidy room turned quickly, their expressions startled.

Terry was the first to recover.

'Sara!' He came to meet her, both hands held out welcomingly. 'So you got here at last? When did you arrive?'

'Yesterday. I came as soon as I knew,' Sara said defensively, sensing an implied rebuke behind his words and not liking it very much.

'I cabled you right away, and sent a follow-up one when you didn't get in touch.'

'I know, but you sent them to my apartment and unfortunately I was away, travelling about the country with Johnnie. I didn't get the cables until I returned. If they'd been sent to the office, someone would have let me know at once.'

'I'm sorry, my dear. It never occurred to me. Anyway, you're here now, and it's good to see you.'

'I'd like to have a talk with you, Terry.'

Sara looked pointedly at the tall, soignée woman

18

who had not spoken since she had come in, and Terry said quickly,

'This is Céleste, Sara. She's in charge of the fashion departments now.'

Sara smiled.

'Hello, Céleste.'

'How do you do, Miss Blake,' Céleste said coldly, then moved towards the door. 'I'll see you later, Terry, when you're free again.'

'Right, Céleste. I'll let you know.'

He waited until the door closed behind her, then put a casual arm around Sara's shoulders.

'It's certainly grand to see you again after all this time. Living in America's done you good, Sara, or maybe it's only me who's forgotten how very pretty you are.' He indicated the chair behind the big desk. 'Come and sit here.'

She shook her head, feeling embarrassed by his fulsome compliment.

'No, thanks, Terry. This one will do for me.'

She sat down in one of the armchairs, trying to fight the wave of aversion which swept over her when she contrasted these expensive and opulent surroundings with what the office had been like when her father was alive.

'Just as you wish,' Terry said casually, and took the chair which she had refused, settling himself into it with an arrogance which was new in Sara's knowledge of him. 'Well now, what do you think of the store? It's quite something, isn't it?'

'It must have cost thousands, Terry. Where did the money come from? I know David sold the house, but even so—it couldn't possibly have paid for all this.'

'It didn't—that's the trouble.'

'You mean, it's not paid for?'

'Exactly.'

She was silent for a moment, then said with a resolute lift of her chin,

'How much is still owing?'

He moved restlessly, flashing her an oblique glance which made her feel even more uneasy.

'We, or more correctly, you and Val, owe Brent Maxwell nearly thirty thousand pounds.'

Sara stared at him in disbelief.

'Thirty thousand pounds? I can't believe it. For what?'

'For everything. You see, as well as owning a wholesale cloth warehouse, he manufactures all kinds of materials. He also has a carpet factory. Then he's a consultant architect, too, so as well as supplying all the furnishings, David also employed him to advise on the alterations.'

'And he hasn't been paid?'

'Apparently not. Since David died he's been putting pressure on us to settle, and we can't do it.'

'Won't the Bank help?'

He laughed.

'Be your age, Sara. We've already got a massive overdraft, secured on the building.'

She stared at him, moistening suddenly dry lips, appalled by the knowledge of how much worse the situation was than anything she had visualised.

'But David told me he'd raised enough money to pay for everything. What's happened to it?'

Terry shrugged.

'How should I know? You'd better ask Brent Maxwell that.'

'You mean he's had it and—'

'Oh, come now, Sara! I didn't say that at all. Don't put words into my mouth.'

No, she thought silently, but that's what you meant to imply. Why? But she could think of no reasonable answer to that question.

'Have you asked him for time to pay?' she said at last.

He laughed shortly.

'Of course. He just says he's waited long enough.'

'But doesn't he understand what it means to us?'

'None better, and he doesn't care. He'll tell you he's in business to make profits, that there's no time for sentiment. Believe me, Sara, there's only one thing to be done. You'll have to sell out. Val agrees with me.'

'Does she? She didn't say anything about it to

me. In fact, she doesn't seem to have understood anything you said to her. Are you sure, Terry?'

He flushed.

'Of course I am. I told her we'd had a very good offer—all debts paid and most of the staff kept on—and she agreed that the best thing to do was to close with it.'

'I see. And what will be left for us? Anything?'

'Naturally, I hope there'll be something,' he began smoothly.

'Rubbish,' she cut in. 'You're not talking to Val now, you're talking to me. Don't forget I've been Johnnie Acton's assistant for nearly three years. I may be only twenty-one, Terry, but there's nothing much you can tell me about the finance of running a business.'

'All right,' he said sulkily. 'So you know it all. Maybe there won't be so very much for you and Val, but I still think the offer I've had is too good to turn down. At least it will keep Blake's open.'

She looked down at her hands, clasped tightly together in her lap, and was surprised at the pain which darted through her at his words. Because the business which her father had built up so lovingly and patiently through sheer hard work was being disposed of as casually as if it was nothing of any moment.

'If these people are willing to buy, they must have faith in the business,' she said at last.

' Oughtn't we to have, too?'

He moved impatiently.

' They've got the money to pour into it. We haven't. Faith by itself will never solve anything.'

' Neither will selling. If we accept this offer, Val will be penniless, won't she?'

His glance shifted away from hers.

' There's no alternative, Sara.'

' I don't accept that. Suppose I go and talk with this Brent Maxwell?'

' Appeal to his better nature, do you mean? You'd be wasting your time, because he hasn't got one. He's as hard as nails. Anyway, what good could come of it? Let me close with this offer, Sara,' he added coaxingly. ' Believe me, it's the only way, if we're to save anything at all from the wreck.'

She shook her head.

' No. Not until I've seen Brent Maxwell,' she said stubbornly.

He got up, the angry colour flooding into his face.

' You must be crazy! What do you hope to gain from it?'

' Time,' she answered quietly. ' Time to think, to make a plan. What's his telephone number?'

For a moment she thought he was going to refuse to tell her and braced herself mentally for an unpleasant battle with him. Then, as suddenly as it had come, the anger which had sharpened his features was gone, and he was his usual charming self again.

'All right, Sara, you must do as you wish.' He pulled a pad towards him and wrote briefly on it. 'There's the number, but I still think you're wasting your time.'

'Perhaps I am, but at least I'm doing something constructive.' She moved towards the door, but turned before she reached it. 'Who's using your old office?'

'Nobody.'

'Then I'll take it over. Please have all the books put in there for me to go through.'

'Now look here, Sara,' he blustered. 'The auditors—'

'I've no doubt they've done their job,' she interrupted. 'Mine is a bit different. If I'm going to make the decision you're pressing for, I've got to know what I'm doing. So see the books are ready for me tomorrow, please.'

He shrugged.

'All right, if that's what you want.'

'Thank you,' she said, and opened the door, closing it firmly behind her.

But she did not walk away at once. Terry's news had come as a shock to her and she had not yet had time to adjust to it, particularly to the knowledge that there would be no money left for Val and Jamie.

24

She pressed her hands together, facing up to the fact that she alone was to blame. She had accepted what David had told her and had been too immersed in the fascinating and interesting life she had been leading in America to give the family business the attention she should have done. She, of all people, should have been aware of what was happening. Johnnie always said she had a nose for trouble, but it seemed to have deserted her in this particular instance, she thought ruefully.

That being so, it was up to her to do all she could to put things right, so that Val and Jamie did not suffer through her neglect. So although everything she had heard so far about Brent Maxwell made her feel very loth to ask him for any favours, there was nothing else she could do.

Unless Johnnie—but she pushed that thought away from her at once. Because he was already deep in a deal which involved millions of dollars and everything he had at that time was tied up in it.

Of course he would help if she asked him, she knew that without question. But she also knew that the smallest thing could upset the balance of this deal on which they had been working, the biggest thing they had ever handled.

No. This time she was on her own. This was her big chance to show what she could do. But first of all she had to see Brent Maxwell. Until she had done that she could not make any plans at all.

She looked around her, getting her bearings, then went along the passage, turning at the end into another one which was vastly different. With its worn linoleum and dark paint it might have been in another world altogether.

Near the end of it she stopped and opened a chipped door which led into the small, unpretentious office which had once been Terry's. She sat down at the desk and lifted the telephone receiver, giving Brent Maxwell's number, her heart thudding nervously against her ribs with trepidation as she waited for the reply.

'Can I speak to Mr Brent Maxwell?' she asked, when at last it came.

'I'll see. Who is calling, please?'

'Sara Blake, of Blake's Store,' she said, and her hand tightened around the receiver when a deep voice said curtly,

'Maxwell here.'

'I'm Sara Blake.'

She paused, annoyed with herself because her voice sounded breathless and very young, more suited to a schoolgirl than a woman who was facing a situation which she had known more than once in America. Only then it had affected strangers, not herself and her family.

'What is it you want?'

'I understand from my manager, Mr White, that

Blake's owes you a considerable amount of money.'

'Yes, that's so.'

'I'd like to talk to you about it.'

'Why? I don't see the necessity. I've made the position quite clear, I think.'

'Perhaps you have.' Her voice was edgy with annoyance at the brusque replies she was receiving. 'But my sister-in-law and I are the owners, not Terry White. You should have seen us.'

She heard him let out his breath in a long-suffering way.

'I did try to see your brother's wife, Miss Blake, but I was told she didn't want to meet me. And you were in America, and hadn't bothered to reply to the cables that had been sent to you.'

Sara felt the hot colour flood into her face, and had to exercise great self-control to stop her voice from trembling with annoyance as she answered him, sharply,

'Well, I'm home now, and I want to discuss the whole situation with you.'

There was silence for a moment, then he said, a note of annoyed resignation very clear in his voice, 'Very well, though you're wasting your own time and mine. And although yours may not be valuable, mine most certainly is.'

She closed her lips tightly on the blistering retort she would have liked to make to this arrogant man, knowing that she could not afford to alienate him when she had to ask him for a favour which was so valuable to her and which she was now sure was not going to be easy to obtain, and only said quietly,

'When can you see me?'

'Tomorrow at eleven o'clock. At the store.'

Suddenly she knew that she did not want to meet him for the first time in the place which Terry, in some obscure way, seemed to have made his own.

'No, not at the store,' she answered quickly. 'I'd like Val, my sister-in-law, to be there. Will you come to the flat?'

'Oh, very well, if you insist. Where is it?'

She gave him the address, trying not to allow the exasperation and irritation at his curtness sound in her voice, a curtness which, in her present ultra-sensitive mood, she interpreted as undisguised boredom because he was going to have to deal with somebody he clearly classed as an unmitigated nuisance.

'I'll be there at eleven. I hope you won't delay me too long, Miss Blake. I'm a very busy man.'

'I won't,' she said, and carefully replaced the receiver, though she would rather have banged it down in anger.

She rubbed her hands over her face, feeling frustrated and very worried indeed. Terry had warned her that she would be wasting her time in appealing to Brent Maxwell, and she knew now that he had been right. After talking with him she would have preferred to have nothing at all to do with him, but she knew that to be impossible.

She had to see him, for Val's sake and for Jamie's. It was their future which was at stake and which must be safeguarded, even though it meant that she must swallow her own pride and sue for favours from this arrogant, impatient man.

CHAPTER III

Sara did not tell Val about the appointment she had made with Brent Maxwell until breakfast time next morning, thinking that her sister-in-law would probably lie awake all night worrying about it. But even so, she was not really prepared for her reaction to the news.

' I won't see him, Sara,' Val cried. ' You've no right to interfere. Terry says you've ruined everything.'

Sara looked at her blankly.

' What are you talking about? Don't you understand, Val? If we sell the business now, there'll probably be no money for you and Jamie.'

' You don't know that. Terry says there will be when everything's fixed up, but if we don't accept this offer, then we'll all be ruined. He's trying to do the best he can for me. You shouldn't meddle in things that don't properly concern you.'

' Don't concern me? You're talking nonsense, Val.' She stopped, restraining herself with an effort, realising that her sister-in-law did not really understand what she was saying. ' When did Terry tell you this?'

' Last night,' Val said sulkily. ' He rang me up quite late after I'd gone to bed. The extension's in my room. I won't see that man, Sara. I won't! Terry says he's awful.'

Sara's lips tightened. So Terry had already tried to sabotage what she was hoping to accomplish. Why should he do that? Why tell her one story and Val another? What did he expect to gain personally from the sale of the store? Money, or perhaps position and power? Though he had surely already achieved the last two aims. Unless she decided to stay in England and take charge.

Suddenly Sara knew this must be the right answer. She had always thought he was ambitious and self-seeking, but had not blamed him for that. Anyone who wanted to get on needed those traits. But while she had no objection to him trying to make sure of his own future, she was not going to allow him to do so at the expense of David's son.

' It's too late to put Brent Maxwell off now, Val, but you needn't see him if you don't want to.'

Val moved impatiently.

' I don't know why you're so against selling, Sara. It was different for David—it was his career. It isn't yours. You'll want to go back to the States and get married. It all seems quite pointless to me.'

Sara's lips tightened as she realised how well Terry had primed her sister-in-law, but she only said quietly,

' I suppose it does, but it's something that goes

deep with me. Ever since I've known anything, I've known about Dad's shop. It's part of my life —just as it was part of David's.'

'Part of David's! That's putting it mildly. It was all his life. I didn't come anywhere near it, I can tell you. He didn't care what he did to me, provided the store was all right. He uprooted me from my lovely house—the house I chose and which my father paid for when we were married. That had to be sacrificed like everything else because he wanted money for his wretched business.'

Sara looked at her in surprise, knowing that for the first time she was hearing the truth from her sister-in-law, and wondering why she had never realised before the depth of her antagonism against David's obsession with the store.

'David told me in one of his letters that you'd suggested you should sell the house and take a rented flat,' she said.

'Me? I did nothing of the kind. He made up his mind to do it and nothing I could say made any difference. Just as he refused to send Jamie to a decent school instead of to one nobody's ever heard of because he went there himself.'

'You can hardly blame him for that, Val.'

'Oh, it's no use talking to you! You think he could do no wrong. You might have changed your mind if you'd had to sit here day after day seeing nobody in this flat while he went off to France to enjoy himself and never once took me with him.'

Sara smiled, knowing that she had now reached the truth of the matter.

'He probably thought you wouldn't be interested in the buying and bargaining he had to do.'

'I wouldn't have bothered about that. I could have enjoyed myself in other ways, but he would never take me. He always said he couldn't afford it,' Val added scornfully.

'It could have been true,' Sara pointed out, thinking that Paris was the last place she would turn her chic and extravagant sister-in-law loose in on her own.

'Nonsense! But even if it was true, then there's all the more reason to take this offer Terry's had. Then I'd have enough money to do what I want, instead of worrying where the next half penny's coming from.'

Sara frowned, hearing a note almost of panic in her voice.

'Are you in any difficulty, Val?' she asked quickly. 'Have you money troubles?'

Val shook her blonde head.

'No, of course not, except as far as we all have money worries—never having enough of it,' she finished, and laughed.

But to Sara her laugh sounded forced and artificial, and she looked at her, wondering if she should press her further to find out the real truth.

Though even as she thought it she realised it would be a waste of time. She knew Val too well. Her father had always shaken his head and said he never knew when she was telling the truth. That she had all the obstinacy of a weak character, and long before she had gone to America Sara had discovered that to be true.

'Then you won't see Brent Maxwell with me?'

'No, I won't. And I might as well tell you now, Sara, that as soon as all David's shares are transferred to me, I'm going to outvote you and sell. Terry says he had by far the majority holding.'

'Then you don't know about the Trust?'

'What Trust?'

'Dad's. He had most of the shares and they were left in trust, first for David and then for David's eldest son. David and I were joint Trustees. Now there's only me.'

'What does that mean?' Val asked suspiciously.

'That I'm the one who administers the Trust on behalf of Jamie.'

Val stared at her in disbelief.

'You mean I get nothing?'

'You'll get David's own shareholding, I think.'

'How many did he have?'

'David and I both held a fifth of the shares each. Dad made no difference between us over that, even though I was eighteen years younger than David.'

'And that's all I get? Is it true? Is it, Sara,

or are you just trying to outmanoeuvre me?'

'You know I wouldn't do that, Val. Won't you change your mind now and see Brent Maxwell with me?'

'No, I will not. I won't talk to him or to anyone. This is just one more thing David's done to me. Why didn't he make things right in his will so that I was the Trustee instead of you? Any other man would have seen that his wife was properly looked after, but not him. Oh, no! Not David Blake!'

'Val, don't say such things! It wasn't David's fault. There was nothing he could do about it. Don't you understand—'

'No, I don't, and I never will. I'm going to my room now. When Maxwell comes see him yourself, and much good may it do you!'

Val rushed out of the room, banging the door behind her, and Sara sighed, feeling depressed and weary. If only she could dismiss her responsibilities as easily as Val seemed to! But she could not. Her training with Johnnie and her own nature made it impossible for her even to consider it for a moment. Though she would have given anything not to have to see this arrogant man and plead with him for the time she needed to tarry and save the business for Jamie and Val. Even though she knew now she would get no thanks for doing so.

She walked restlessly across the thick off-white

close carpeting, automatically straightening a brilliantly coloured satin cushion on the luxurious sofa, and wondered for the first time who had paid for all the expensive furniture in this big penthouse flat, and whether the cost of it might not be included in the debt which Brent Maxwell said was due to him, whose coming she awaited with so much trepidation.

Though when at last the door bell rang just as eleven o'clock was striking musically from the French clock on the bracket in the sitting room, she gave no sign of her inner feelings as she answered it.

'Miss Blake? Good morning. I'm Brent Maxwell.'

She looked up at the tall man whose eyes met hers without friendliness, and had to adjust her ideas.

For he was nothing like the image she had dreamed up of him. Here was no ogre, no hard business tycoon as she had imagined. Instead she saw deep-set blue eyes in a face with sensitive lines engraved in it. Eyes which, though unsmiling at that moment, were set in laughter lines.

'Yes, I'm Sara Blake,' she said. 'Please come in.'

She led the way into the sitting room and saw his eyes look quickly round him, as though assessing the cost of what he saw, and thought with relief that probably he had had no hand in the furnishing of

36

it.

'Would you like something to drink?'

'No, thank you. I've very little time to spare, so let's just hear what you've got to say and cut the formalities, shall we?'

Her lips tightened at his curt words and she looked at him with annoyance and dislike.

'That suits me. I don't wish to keep you a moment longer than you want to stay. Terry White told me yesterday that you intend to ruin us all in order to get the money you say is owing to you. Is that true?'

He frowned, his eyes wary.

'Basically, though it's not the way I'd have put it.'

Sara made an impatient gesture.

'That's beside the point. I want to know the truth. Does our business owe you thirty thousand pounds, Mr Maxwell, and do you intend to wait no longer for repayment?'

'Yes,' he said shortly. 'I've waited more than a year now, and while David was alive I agreed not to press for payment. But that's all changed, since his death. You may not understand why—'

'Give me the benefit of some sense,' she interrupted angrily. 'I'm not completely inexperienced, you know. I've been working in the States for a finance house for nearly three years. There's very little you can tell me that I wouldn't understand.'

He raised his eyebrows.

' In that case why bother to see me? You ought to know that I'm doing the only possible thing under the circumstances.'

' I'd have thought it was obvious.'

' Not to me, and I'm not considered to be particularly obtuse. If you're so well versed in financial matters you ought to know that when I lent money to Blake's I was backing a man in whom I had trust, who I expected to forge ahead. Now he's gone, there's nothing left for me to do but make sure I'm paid in full as quickly as possible.'

She coloured at the weary note in his voice and would have given anything at that moment to walk away and leave him there, without asking him for the help that only he could give. But she knew she dared not do it, that she was indulging in dangerous wishful thinking.

Though that realisation only served to deepen the dislike she had felt for him from the moment she had spoken with him on the telephone.

' Well, Miss Blake?' he asked impatiently. ' What is it you want to say to me?'

' I want you to give me time,' she said, without wrapping up the request in flowery language. ' So that I can find out what's been happening at Blake's.'

' What good will that do? Whatever has happened can't affect the result now. It must be obvious to you, if you are as knowledgeable as you claim to be, that it would be better to go into liquidation voluntarily or to sell as a going concern.'

'Perhaps, but I don't want to do either of those things.'

'Why not?'

She hesitated, wondering if she could tell him the real truth, if he would understand the deep feelings which were driving her. The reluctance to see all her father had striven for and built up gone as if they had never been, and Jamie and Val reduced, perhaps, to penury.

He frowned, looking at her with suspicion.

'Don't try to hide anything from me,' he said sharply. 'I've got to know the whole truth if I'm to make a decision which involves my company.'

'I don't want to hide anything from you. I'll be quite frank with you. David sold up his home, raised every bit of money he could, to pay for all the alterations and furnishings, yet you say you haven't been paid anything. So what's happened to the money, Mr Maxwell?'

He looked at her in disbelief, the lines beside his mouth deepening in anger.

'How dare you? Are you accusing me of taking your brother's money when he was alive, and asking for it again now he's dead?'

For a moment she quailed before his anger, then thrust that sudden stab of fear aside, knowing that she was right to ask that question.

'It's no use getting annoyed, Mr Maxwell. I think it's a reasonable thing to ask.'

'Do you? Well, I don't. Do you realise what you're saying? Do you?'

She felt the colour recede from her face at his angry words, but stood her ground, determined not to be intimidated by him.

'You're deliberately misunderstanding me.'

His lips set sternly.

'Then you're not accusing me of embezzlement?'

'Of course not. I'm only trying to find out where this money's gone to, if it hasn't been paid to you.'

'Then you'd better examine the firm's books.'

'I intend to, as soon as I can. Will you do as I ask, Mr Maxwell? Give me time to investigate?'

His lips curved in a reluctant smile which altered the whole character of his face.

'Well, if you don't take the prize for complete illogicality! Handing out insults to me one minute, then expecting favours from me the next. Why should I consider you?'

She found herself answering his smile reluctantly, feeling her resolution not to give way to this man weakening in the face of his sudden, unexpected charm.

'You've just told me I'm illogical. Do you expect me to have a reason?' she asked lightly.

He did not answer immediately, looking keenly at her as if trying to read her mind.

'Take my advice,' he said at last. 'Cut your losses.'

'No, I won't do that, not until I've had time to look into things. That's all I'm asking for—time, to do the best I can for Val and Jamie.'

'You won't succeed.'

'Perhaps not, but I still want to try. Will you let me?'

'Is your sister-in-law in agreement with you?'

She coloured under his steady gaze.

'She doesn't properly understand—'

'She wants to sell, does she?' he asked drily.

'I've told you, she doesn't understand that if we do sell there may be little or nothing left for her.'

'What if she outvotes you in a showdown, Sara Blake? Have you thought of that?'

'Yes, but she can't do it. My father held three-fifths of the shares and they passed in Trust to David and then to Jamie. David and I were the Trustees. Now there's only me. So you see, I'm in control, not Val.'

'I see. Does she know?'

'I told her this morning.'

He was silent for a time, frowning down at his clasped hands, and she watched him, silently willing him to give her the right answer, the answer she wanted.

'Well,' she said at last when the silence became unbearable. 'What's your answer?'

'I'll do as you ask, Sara Blake.' He looked at her steadily out of keen blue eyes. 'I'll give you three months to get to know the business and put things right if you can.'

'Three months?' she echoed in dismay. 'It isn't long enough. I'll never do it.'

He got up abruptly.

'That's my offer, take it or leave it. If you're only half as good as you say you are, it ought to be plenty of time. And I'll give you all the help I can.'

She felt a wave of anger shiver through her and wished passionately that she could give way to it, could throw back this man's ridiculous offer in his face. But she did not dare. She had to accept it because it was her only hope, even while she despaired of carrying out all her plans in such a short time.

'All right, I'll accept. Thank you,' she said, with an effort.

'Good. Au revoir, then, Sara Blake.'

'Goodbye,' she answered with emphasis, telling herself that she would have to be in very great difficulties indeed before she took up his offer of help, but she was uneasily aware of the amused look he gave her as he opened the front door.

She stood where she was when the door closed with a decisive click behind him, feeling panic rising within her. She had accepted his terms and somehow she had to succeed, without the help he had offered her and which she was too proud to accept.

And in addition to undertaking an almost impossible task, she would not be able to go back to America, to Johnnie. He was relying on her to come back and help him to put through the complicated deal they had been working on when she had heard of David's death, and she was going to let him down. Not only that, but she was going to miss him badly.

Dear Johnnie, so loved and so needed. She could see him in her mind's eye, his thick fair hair falling over his forehead, his eyes bright with enthusiasm and eagerness, and knew an intense longing to be with him, to draw strength from him.

Instead she had only Brent Maxwell, that difficult, strange man, as unlike Johnnie as anyone could be. If only she need never see him again, but remembering the amused look in his eyes and his voice saying 'Au revoir', she knew there was little hope of that.

She had invited him into her life, and now had the uneasy feeling that however much she might dislike it, he had every intention of staying there.

43

CHAPTER IV

Sara went into the store next morning by the staff entrance, joining the others who were doing the same thing, hurrying or dawdling according to their natures. Some of them looked at her curiously, while others pushed past unseeingly, snatching their cards from the rack and clocking on with a sublime disregard for anyone or anything.

They all seemed to know each other and called out cheerful greetings. Sara felt very lonely as she went quickly upstairs to the office she had requisitioned, wondering if Terry would have put the firm's books in it or whether she was going to have to battle with him to get them. But when she pushed open the door of the dark little office and went in, switching on the light, she saw that she need not have worried. On the scarred desk was a pile of ledgers.

So she had misjudged him, she thought, as she hung up her coat in the cupboard. He was going to co-operate with her after all. Yet under the feeling of thankfulness that she was not to be faced with a struggle to get the information she wanted, there was one of faint surprise at his easy capitulation.

She sat down at the desk and opened the first

ledger, but before she could do more than glance at it, Terry came in.

'Hi, Sara. You're early. Got everything you need?'

'I haven't really looked yet, but thank you for letting me have the books so promptly.'

'Think nothing of it. I had them put in as soon as Val rang to tell me Maxwell had been to see you and you'd managed to talk him round. I expected you to come in yesterday.'

Sara pushed back her thick honey-gold hair from her forehead.

'I meant to, but Val wasn't a bit well in the afternoon, so I stayed with her. When did she ring you?'

'Before lunch.'

'I see,' Sara said slowly, remembering her sister-in-law's attack of hysterics and her insistence afterwards that Sara should not leave her. Yet before that she had been capable of ringing Terry up and letting him know what had happened. And for the first time she wondered just how real Val's attack of nerves had been. 'Did she tell you about the shares?'

'Yes, though I already knew that. Don't forget I worked with your father and David for a good long time.'

Sara frowned, wondering if he was telling the truth or if he was trying to hide what he had been

45

planning.

'If you knew that, why did you try to persuade Val to sell, telling her she would be able to outvote me?' she asked, determined to find the answer to that problem.

'Nonsense, Sara, I did nothing of the kind. I merely told her the real situation. You're not suggesting I should have hidden the truth from her, are you, unpalatable though it is.'

She coloured at the implied rebuke in his words.

'No, of course not. I only wondered why you should have said she would have all the shares and be in control.'

'I didn't. Val must have misunderstood me. You said yourself that she didn't seem to know what I'd been talking about.' He looked at her speculatively. 'Have you thought what you'll do if Jamie doesn't want to come into the business when he's old enough, Sara? If, say, he decides he'd rather be a doctor or a lawyer or something?'

'I'll face that problem when it comes.'

'You may be sorry when you've spent years toiling to pull the business round, and all for nothing.'

'That's a risk I've got to take. Up to now he's always seemed keen enough.'

'Boys have been known to change their minds.' She sighed.

'I know that. What I must make sure of is that there's still a business for him to inherit, if he does

46

want it.'

'And if he doesn't? What then?'

'We'll have to sell, I suppose, but maybe we'll be able to drive a better bargain for us all.'

He flicked her cheek with a casual finger.

'Always the incurable optimist, Sara, but I love you for it. Anyway, I didn't come through to talk about that. I want you to come round the store with me to see what we've been doing and to meet some of the staff.'

It took a long time to make the tour of the store. Terry showed her everything, and she talked for a while to a number of the staff. They seemed friendly enough, yet somehow Sara could sense a constraint, almost an antagonism among them, particularly among the departmental heads. Yet how could that be? They did not know enough about her to be antagonistic towards her, because without exception they had joined the firm after she had left to go to America.

She said as much to Terry as they walked towards the model gown department, and he shrugged lightly.

'I suppose they feel unsettled, Sara, and tend to blame you, as part of the Blake family. That often happens when staff feel there may be a change in the air.'

'I suppose you're right. Terry, everybody I've met today has been new. I hoped I might see some

47

of the old friends I used to know. What's happened to them all?'

'I expect they've left from time to time. The usual wastage, you know. We're none of us getting any younger.'

She frowned, looking back over the past three years, remembering the staff she had known then.

'Perhaps, yet I don't think they were so old, Terry. I doubt if any of them were much more than fifty. Yet they've all gone. It seems strange to me.'

'I don't see why it should,' he said indifferently. 'People get set in their own ways and resist changes. And there've been a lot of changes here in one way and another, as you can see.'

'Yes. Is there only Mollie left?'

'How did you know she was still here?'

'I met her that first day when I came to see you.'

She stopped, thinking suddenly how short a time had elapsed since she had come back from America. Yet it seemed to her that she had been home for weeks. Almost as if she had never been away.

It wasn't her life now that was strange, but rather that the life she had spent in America during the last three years had become vague and dreamlike, as if it had never been.

Just as at that moment it was an effort for her to conjure up the image of Johnnie, who had been close to her every day during that time.

'Well now, this is the real *pièce de résistance*.'

Terry's voice broke in on her thoughts and she pushed them resolutely into the background of her mind, concentrating once again on the task of trying to assess the cost of the changes that had taken place and what effect they had had on store sales.

She looked around her, seeing the thick pile carpet, the catwalk surrounded by gilt and velvet chairs, the huge windows shrouded in white nylon curtains, the brilliance of the chandeliers reflected in the mirrors lining the walls, and gave her brother full marks for his foresight and originality.

Whatever it had cost, and there could be no doubt that the cost had been great, it was in itself an achievement and gave a final cachet to the new look for Blake's Store.

'Good morning, Miss Blake.'

She turned quickly at Céleste's cool greeting and smiled into the tall woman's expressionless face.

'Good morning. This is really a very beautiful room. How often do you have dress shows?'

'Two or three times a week to invited people. You know we make gowns for the trade as well as for individual customers?'

'Are the workrooms still in the same place?'

'Yes, although very much bigger now.'

'I'd like to see them.'

'You won't find them very interesting, Sara. David didn't get round to doing them up.'

49

'Still, I may as well visit them, then I've had a look at all departments, haven't I?'

'Just as you please. Come along, then.'

He began to walk along the corridor, but stopped when Céleste called imperiously,

'Just a moment, Mr White. Could I have a word with you?'

'Of course, Céleste. I won't be a moment,' he added to Sara, and walked quickly back to where Céleste waited for him.

Sara watched them talking to each other in low tones, too quietly for her to hear what they were saying, only part of her mind concentrated on them.

'All right, do that,' Terry said in a much louder voice, and came briskly back to Sara. 'Sorry about that, my dear, but these little problems do arise. This way.'

They walked to the end of the passage, then climbed a flight of uncarpeted stairs leading to the attic rooms. As Terry had said, nothing had been spent on them and they looked dingy and rather grim.

But when he pushed open a door in the narrow passageway, the whole picture changed. Because here was all the colour and brightness which she had known in her father's time.

She stood in the doorway, her dark eyes shining with memories, though in those days there had been nothing like the number of machinists who

50

were employed now. They sat in long rows, the hum of their powered machines filling the air. Sara had never seen so many collected in one room in her life. What a change from the modest half dozen which was the most her father had ever employed, even in his most flourishing period.

She turned impulsively to Terry.

'It's terrific! How on earth do you keep them all busy?'

'Very easily. We do a lot more work now, making for the trade. Come through to the other room where the hand sewers are and where all the model gowns are made.'

He led the way down the machine room, none of the sewers stopping their work as they passed, to Sara's surprise.

'Well, time's money to them,' Terry said, when she commented on this. 'They're on bonus, you see, and earn colossal amounts every week. Which means we have to pay the hand sewers comparable salaries, otherwise we couldn't get them.'

Sara walked slowly past the sewing women, seeing the tables covered with beautiful materials, many of them being exquisitely embroidered, stopping now and again to admire the work being done. Here the women had time to speak to her, to explain what they were doing.

'Who thinks up the designs?' she asked.

'David used to. He was in close touch with the

Paris houses, of course, but he always gave the designs the Blake touch.'

'What will you do now?'

'We're all right for this season, but after that I'm not sure. We'll probably have to employ a designer, but it isn't going to be easy to find one. Céleste and I have already started to make some enquiries, and I'll probably go over to Paris soon to see if there's anybody there we can use.'

'That's going to be quite expensive, isn't it?' Sara said, then her eyes lighted up as Mollie came through a door at the end of the room. 'Oh, here's Mollie. How are you? I'm glad I haven't missed you.'

'Good morning, Miss Blake, Mr White.'

Mollie's voice was as expressionless as her face and Sara looked at her in surprise, hardly recognising the warm, friendly person she had met earlier.

'What's wrong?' she asked, with concern. 'Are you feeling all right?'

'Of course. I'm very busy just at present, so if you'll excuse me—'

Sara stared after her in astonishment as she went quickly through the room and into the other one which Sara and Terry had just left, then turned to him, a question on her lips which was destined never to be asked. Because as she looked at him it occurred to her with startling suddenness that

Mollie had snubbed her only because she was with Terry. And that thought perplexed her very much indeed.

Because if it was true, it must mean that Mollie was afraid of him, yet why should she be? Terry seemed affable enough with her and with all the members of the staff. Then she remembered. Only Mollie seemed to be left of those who had worked at Blake's when her father was alive, who knew the old régime. Was she really so afraid that now David was dead Terry might find some excuse to be rid of her, too?

Well, if that was so, then somehow, she told herself, she would make sure that Mollie's job at Blake's was safe. Even though everything that was happening was tying her more securely to England; was making it that much more difficult for her to go back to the States and Johnnie.

'Well, now you've seen everything, Sara,' Terry said briskly as they walked back to the office. 'What about coming out to lunch with me?'

She looked at him, her eyes still mirroring her troubled thoughts.

'No, thank you, Terry. I meant to get through such a lot of work this morning and I've done nothing.'

'I wouldn't say that, my dear. You've seen the store and know now where all the money's gone. And you'll have to take lunch somewhere.'

' It's too early yet.'

' Not at all. It's long gone twelve, you know. You haven't realised how quickly the time has been passing. Please come,' he added coaxingly, ' just to show you forgive me for trying to persuade you to sell the business.'

She laughed.

' All right, Terry. Give me a few minutes to wash and tidy myself up a bit.'

' As long as you like. I'll meet you at the main entrance. See you, my dear.'

He left her at the office and she went in, doing automatically all the things necessary, her mind still concentrated on what she had seen that day, trying to sort out all the impressions she had received while going round the store.

But it was no use. Everything was too close for her to assess it in a sensible way and in the end she had to acknowledge that she was probably doing the right thing in going out to lunch with Terry. Perhaps after she had been away from the store for a while she might be able to get what she had seen and learned into perspective so that it would be of help when she began to make her analysis of the firm's ledgers.

She looked at her watch, realising that she had taken longer than she had intended to, and picked up her handbag from the desk before running out of the office and down the stairs to the main entrance.

Terry was waiting for her with a taxi.

'I was just coming to find you,' he said, opening the door for her, then getting in and sitting down beside her. 'I was beginning to think you'd stood me up.'

'As if I would! I'm sorry I was so long, Terry. I've no excuse, really.'

'That's all right.' He smiled down at her. 'Now you're here, will you promise me one thing?'

'If I can,' she said cautiously.

'You can. I want us to have our meal without once mentioning Blake's, to forget all that's happened and just enjoy ourselves. That's easy enough, surely?'

She put out her hand impulsively to him.

'Of course it is, Terry. Thank you. You've been very kind to me today and I appreciate it.'

He put his own lightly over hers.

'It's fatally easy for me to be kind to you, my dear. It always was. Don't you remember how one look from those big dark eyes of yours made me like putty in your hands? They still have that power,' he finished ruefully.

She made some reply, flustered by his extravagant words, and was glad when the taxi drew up at that moment in front of the restaurant he had chosen and she could withdraw her hand from his, beginning to wish that she had not come out with him.

She did not like or welcome this sudden and unexpected change in him and yet was loth to upset him when he was trying to be kind to her, by letting him see that she had no wish to be reminded of those years when she had hero-worshipped her father's good-looking young assistant.

Though she need not have worried. Terry said nothing further to embarrass her but was a charming companion, interested in hearing about her life in America and making no reference at all to Blake's, so that she too was able to keep her part of the bargain they had made.

It was as they were drinking coffee that she first looked at her wrist watch and said with a startled exclamation,

'Heavens, it's almost three o'clock, Terry. Do you realise how long we've taken over our lunch?'

'Yes, but I hoped you hadn't.'

'We should have been back at the store ages ago. You'll have been wanted there.'

He laughed.

'Oh, I don't often get the chance to play hookey, my dear, and it's worth taking a bit longer over lunch to see you lose that worried look. Mind you don't let it come back,' he added. 'You look a lot prettier without it.'

She coloured.

'Maybe, but we really ought to go back now.'

'Just as you like. I'll meet you downstairs. Ask

the commissionaire to call a taxi, will you?'

The taxi was waiting when he rejoined Sara and they were almost silent until they reached the store. She waited while Terry paid the driver, then they walked in together through the imposing main entrance.

Sara stopped just inside the automatic doors and said, gratefully,

'Thank you, Terry, for a very enjoyable time. You were quite right—I needed an hour or two away from it all. I'd been getting things out of proportion, letting them get on top of me.'

He put his hands on her shoulders, his fingers tightening comfortingly.

'I'm glad to help, Sara love. We must do this again. What about having a meal and doing a show with me one evening?'

She hesitated, not knowing what answer to give to this unexpected invitation, but before she could say anything a voice behind her said furiously,

'Next time you make an appointment with me, Miss Blake, please see you're there to keep it!'

She whirled round, looking into Brent Maxwell's angry eyes in astonishment.

'What are you talking about? What do you mean?' she demanded.

'Don't play the innocent with me,' he said contemptuously. 'Perhaps it's your way of trying to look important, to bring me here and keep me waiting to suit your convenience. Well, it doesn't work that way with me. Remember that in future.'

She stared after him as he went quickly past the counter to the main door, hardly able to understand what she had heard. Then as she saw the interested glances of the assistants who had easily heard everything he had said in his deep, carrying voice, the brilliant colour flooded into her cheeks and her puzzlement changed to anger.

'How dare he speak to me like that! I don't know what he's talking about. I made no appointment with him.'

'Are you sure, Sara?'

'Of course I'm sure. I wouldn't be likely to forget that. I'm not so stupid, as I'd have told him if he'd given me the chance. He's—oh, he's self-opinionated and arrogant, and I wish I didn't have to have anything to do with him!'

'Well, there's no need for you to. I hate to say I told you so, but you've got to admit that I did warn you about him. Why won't you be sensible, Sara, and do what I advise, then you need never see him again.'

She shook her head.

'I can't do that, Terry, no matter how much I want to.' She looked round suddenly, seeing again the covert interest the nearby staff were taking in their conversation and said quietly, 'We can't talk here. Let's go up to the office.'

She walked over to the escalator and he followed, saying nothing more until they paused outside the room she was using. Then as she turned the door handle he put his hand on hers.

'Just a minute, Sara. I'm sorry our very pleasant lunch had to end like this. And you didn't answer my question. Will you come out with me one evening?'

She smiled at him.

'Yes, I will. Thanks, Terry,' she said, then looked round quickly as Céleste's cold voice said,

'Mrs David called you, Miss Blake. She wants you to go home at once.'

'Why? What's happened?'

'She didn't tell me, but she seemed very upset. I could hardly make out what she said, she was crying so much.'

Sara looked at Terry, the worry back in her eyes again.

'I must go to her, Terry. I can't think what can have gone wrong—'

'I'll call a taxi for you. Go down to the main door and wait there, Sara. It'll be quicker that way.'

'Thank you. I'll do that,' she said gratefully, and hurried back down the stairs, the other two standing together and watching her until she was out of sight.

CHAPTER V

Sara had not been waiting long when the taxi drew up, and she spent the next twenty minutes until she reached the flat worrying and wondering about her sister-in-law, imagining all kinds of calamities, so that Val's trouble seemed almost an anti-climax at first.

' Here you are at last! ' Val said peevishly when she hurried into the flat. ' You've taken your time. I thought you'd never come.'

' Terry took me out to lunch and I only got your message when I got back to the store. What's happened, Val? What's gone wrong?'

' Terry took you out to lunch? Well, I must say that's rich after all he's——' She broke off, pressing her lips together as if sorry she had said so much, and with a dramatic gesture held out an envelope to Sara, the recorded delivery label standing out starkly against its whiteness.

Sara took out the letter it contained and read it, her heart sinking as she did so.

' Val,' she said at last, ' is this really the rent of the flat? But it's extortionate,' she went on as her sister-in-law nodded. ' We can't possibly afford to go on living here. No wonder it's six months in arrears. You should never have let David come here.'

'I knew you'd blame me,' Val said shrilly. 'As if I could have stopped him! He never told me anything. I'd no idea how much it cost and he always said we'd plenty of money.'

'But this much for rent!'

Val moved impatiently.

'It's not as bad as that, Sara. I'm sure your apartment in America cost a lot more.'

'Yes, but it was furnished.'

'And so is this, partly. Of course, we brought some furniture of our own, too.'

Sara looked at her, the worry in her eyes deepening.

'You mean if we have to leave here we've got to refurnish as well?'

'Yes, but I don't want to leave. I like it here.'

'You may do, but we simply can't afford it. Don't you understand, Val? Everything's different now.'

She saw the tears gather in Valerie's eyes and knew a momentary impatience as she wailed,

'Why did this have to happen to me! I'm sure I've never done anything to deserve it. I won't leave here and go to live in some poky little hole of a place. It's not fair to me or to Jamie.'

'It needn't be poky. Don't you see, Val—' Sara began, then stopped, realising it was useless to try and make her sister-in-law see reason at that moment. Perhaps later, when she had had time to get used to the idea, she might be more willing to consider it rationally and favourably. 'Never mind. Let's forget it, shall we?' she went on. 'I'll go and make some tea for us. We both need it, don't we?'

She went into the kitchen on the words, glad to get away from Val for a few minutes, and as she made the tea and set the trolley, the worried frown was back between her eyes.

It had been bad enough coming home to find the family business on the point of bankruptcy. It made things even worse to discover that even in his private life David had managed to involve himself and his family in debts and difficulties.

What other things was she going to find out, what other shocks might in in store for her? she wondered unhappily as she pushed the trolley into the sitting room.

The tea and perhaps the knowledge that she had sloughed off her worries on to Sara's shoulders seemed to revive Val, and she was chatting quite amiably to Sara when the door bell rang. She stiffened in her chair, the fear back in her eyes.

'Who can that be? Do you think it's the police? Or a debt collector?' Then as Sara got up to answer the bell, she clutched at her desperately. 'Don't go, Sara. Let them ring.'

Sara released herself from that convulsive grip

and said gently,

'Nonsense, Val. It's no one like that. Why should it be? It's probably somebody who's come to the wrong apartment.'

But when she opened the door she found that they were both wrong.

'You!' she said. 'What do you want?'

'To see you,' Brent Maxwell replied with equal brevity. 'I'll come in if I may.'

He did not wait for her to agree but stepped into the small hall, closing the door behind him.

'How dare you force yourself in here!' Sara said fiercely. 'I don't want to see you—'

'Who is it, Sara?'

'It's Brent Maxwell.'

She looked round as Val came hesitantly into the hall, then sighed in exasperation as her sister-in-law took one look at the tall man standing just inside the door and burst into tears, rushing across to her bedroom without another word.

Brent looked after her in surprise.

'What's wrong with her? It's the first time the sight of me has made anyone cry!'

'You astonish me. The way you talked to me this afternoon, I should think you're used to reducing everyone to nervous wrecks.'

He smiled.

'But evidently not you, Sara. You're made of sterner stuff, aren't you?'

'Never mind that! What have you come here for?'

'To apologise to you,' he answered, to her complete astonishment.

'To apologise? You?'

'Yes. I think I did you an injustice, but at the time I was too annoyed to accept the fact that you didn't expect me. You didn't ask me to call, did you?'

'No,' she said briefly, so taken aback by an apology from this arrogant man that she was quite incapable of saying any of the cutting things she had thought of.

He frowned.

'Someone did, however, and it was a woman's voice. It certainly sounded like you, yet—' He stopped, his eyes intent, then went on abruptly, 'I want to talk to you, Sara.'

'You'd better come in here, then,' she said reluctantly, and led the way into the sitting room. 'Sit down, won't you.'

'Thank you. What's the matter with Mrs David?'

'She's a bit upset.'

'So I noticed, not being stupid. Does she always dissolve into tears when somebody unexpected calls?'

'No, of course not.' Sara frowned worriedly, forgetting for a moment how much she disliked this man and succumbing to the urge to share her troubles with somebody else. 'We've had a letter from the agents today telling us that unless we pay the arrears of rent we'll have to leave this apartment. Naturally she's upset about that.'

'Because you can't pay?'

'Partly, and partly because this seems to be the last link she has with David.'

She stopped, vexed with herself because of the tremor in her voice which she had been unable to control.

He looked at her sharply.

'What else is bothering you? You may as well tell me,' he added as she made a gesture of negation. 'If you don't, I'll find out somehow.'

'It's nothing—just that I wish I was sure this was the only debt we'll have to face. And while I don't mind leaving here, it's a furnished apartment and it won't be so easy to find another one at a price we can afford.'

'I see. If you like, Sara, I'll pay off the arrears and continue to pay the rent of this place until you can find somewhere suitable and cheaper.'

She got quickly to her feet, the colour rushing into her face.

'You will not! We owe you too much already.'

He flicked the letter he had picked up disparagingly.

'This amount will make very little difference to

the total.'

'Suppose we never manage to repay you?' she countered.

'You will,' he answered calmly. 'One way or another.'

She looked at him suspiciously.

'You mean you'll force us into bankruptcy if we don't?'

'I didn't say that, but if you like to think it, that suits me. It should suit you, too, because if I do intend to push things to that extreme, you shouldn't mind adding a few more pounds to the bill.'

She took an angry turn around the room, then came to stand in front of him, looking him fearlessly in the eyes.

'No, I won't do it.'

He frowned.

'I can't see what your objection is, unless of course you've made up your mind not to accept any favours from me. And if that is really your reason,' he added with devastating candour, 'then I think it's a stupid one, considering you've already begged me to grant you a favour already.'

'Oh, you—' she began, then stopped, feeling completely helpless, knowing there was nothing she could say.

Because what he said was quite true, but that knowledge only made her dislike him all the more.

He laughed suddenly, though without mirth.

'I see I'm to have the usual reward of the person to whom someone is beholden,' he said grimly.

She coloured, acknowledging to herself the truth of his words, but denying it hotly to him.

'That isn't why I dislike you.'

He raised his eyebrows.

'You've some other reason? May I know what it is?'

'Yes—no— Oh, why do you always try to put me in the wrong?'

'I wasn't aware that I did. You're too sensitive, Sara. You need to grow another skin. How did you get on at the store today?'

She blinked at him, taken aback by the sudden change of subject.

'Get on? In what way?'

'You said you were going to start examining the books. Did you have any trouble getting them?' he explained patiently.

'Oh, I see. No. They were already in the office when I arrived.'

He seemed surprised but did not say anything, and after a moment she asked,

'Why? Did you think I would have?'

He nodded.

'I thought it possible. I'm glad for your sake I was wrong. How far did you get?'

She hesitated, then said reluctantly,

'I didn't even begin. Terry came in before I could do so. He wanted to take me round the store to show me all the alterations that have been made. We talked to some of the staff and that took up quite a bit of time.'

She stopped, remembering the impression of unrest, almost of antagonism she had sensed, and wondered if she ought to mention it to this man, then decided not to.

Because there was nothing she could really put her finger on. Nothing but a vague impression which possibly had no foundation in fact but might be an extension of her own feeling of insecurity.

She was aroused from her thoughts by his sudden question.

'What is it, Sara? What's troubling you?'

'Nothing,' she said quickly. 'Nothing at all.'

He looked at her penetratingly, and she said hurriedly,

'Afterwards Terry took me out to lunch and when we came back there was a message from Val asking me to come home at once.'

'I see,' he said slowly, then sat silently, staring in front of him as if he had forgotten she was there.

He roused himself at last.

'So even though the books were there you were effectively stopped from working on them.'

'I'm sure that wasn't Terry's reason—'

'Are you? Anyway, thank you for being so
68

frank with me, Sara. I'll take this letter with me, if I may, and see if I can stave this particular creditor off for a little while. If I hear of anywhere suitable for you to live, I'll let you know.'

'That's kind of you, but I'd rather you didn't trouble,' she began, then was relieved when at that moment the telephone shrilled out.

Because she did not really know what to say to him, this man whom she was so determined to dislike and who repaid her by being so thoughtful and so kind.

As she lifted the receiver she was almost tempted to apologise to him for the way she had treated him, then as the operator said, 'I have a call for Miss Sara Blake from New York. Is she available?' everything else was forgotten in the happiness of knowing that she was going to talk to Johnnie.

'Johnnie!' she said as she heard his well-remembered voice, as clear as if he was in the same room. 'It's lovely to hear from you. How are you getting on without me?'

'Terrible, honey. Say, what's the idea, sending me a cable like that? Fourteen days is all I allowed you, and I reckon to see you back here at the end of that.'

She laughed ruefully.

'I can't do it, Johnnie. Everything's in such a mess over here, you've no idea. I've got to stay because there isn't anyone else to see to things.'

'And what about me? What about our job?'

'I wish I could fly right back to you, Johnnie, but I can't. You'll have to let me have three months—'

'I will not. If you don't come back here I'll come over and get you.'

'I wish you would! I'd love to see you come walking in through the door. I miss you and, oh, Johnnie, I need you. You don't know how much!'

When they had said goodbye she cradled the receiver, her eyes bright with the happiness of talking to Johnnie, of hearing from him how much she was wanted, after the unhappy experiences she had had since coming to England.

In the excitement of talking to him she had completely forgotten Brent Maxwell, and she jumped when he said coldly,

'A friend of yours, Sara?'

'Oh! I'd forgotten you were there. Yes, it was Johnnie, Johnnie Acton, my boss in America.'

'Your boss? I'm sorry. I must have misunderstood.'

She coloured at his caustic tone.

'I suppose you mean you think we're too friendly. Well, let me tell you something, Brent Maxwell. There's none of this boss/employee nonsense about Johnnie and me.'

'So I noticed! I didn't mean to denigrate American informality. On the contrary, I admire it.'

She could feel the colour mounting hotly into her face under his steady gaze and turned away, walking over to the door and opening it.

'I know exactly what you mean,' she said quietly. 'Now, if you'll excuse me I've got a meal to prepare.'

'Certainly I will. I can tell when I'm not wanted.' He went over to her and before she could move, took her chin in his fingers, tilting up her face towards him. 'Your trouble is that you take offence too easily, my girl. You want to watch that temper of yours.'

For a moment he smiled down into her angry eyes, then let go of her chin and brought his finger gently down her cheek.

'Au revoir, Sara. Until tomorrow,' he said, and was gone before she had time to tell him exactly what she thought of him and his opinions.

She stood where he had left her, one hand against the cheek he had touched, angry with herself because she had allowed him to have the final word.

He was opinionated and arrogant, she told herself fiercely, as she slammed in and out of cupboards and refrigerator, assembling the food for their evening meal. He badly needed putting in his place, that was for sure, and she hoped that one day before very long she would have the opportunity to do it.

She touched her face, feeling again his finger

as it had gently stroked it, then snatched up the dish towel and angrily scrubbed her cheek with it, as if by doing so she could remove every remembrance of him from her mind.

CHAPTER VI

When the meal was ready Sara called Val, who came out of her bedroom wearing a very lovely pale pink negligé which, to Sara's eyes, looked as if it had cost a great deal of money. But then who would wear expensive clothes, she asked herself, trying to forget the niggling worry that perhaps this, as well as many other things was not paid for, if not the wife of the owner of the store?

' Has he gone? What did he want, Sara?' Val asked as soon as she came into the dining alcove.

' Just to talk about some financial details,' Sara replied easily. ' That's a gorgeous outfit, Val. It suits you.'

Her sister-in-law looked down at herself complacently.

' Yes, isn't it? David brought it back with him from Paris a few months ago.'

Sara looked at her quickly, noting that for the first time Val had spoken of David without her eyes filling with tears, and hoped that this meant she was beginning to recover from the shock of his tragic death.

' What sort of financial things did he talk about?' Val asked as they began to eat.

' All kinds.' Sara hesitated, wondering if she

73

should tell Val of Brent's offer to help them, and decided that now, when she seemed to be in a fairly placid mood, might be the right moment. ' He's taken away the letter from the agent and says he'll see to it for us.'

Val's eyes brightened.

' Oh, good! Then we can stay here. How clever of you to get him to do that, Sara.'

' He's only going to see if he can get us time to pay.'

' Pooh, nonsense! I don't believe that.'

Sara stared at her.

' You mean—he's going to pay the bill?'

' Of course.'

' But we can't let him do that.' She pushed back her chair. ' I'll ring him up and stop him—'

' Don't be silly, Sara. Why shouldn't he pay it?'

' Because he's got nothing to do with us, that's why. And we already owe him enough without adding to it.'

Val shrugged.

' He'll get paid one day, and if it means we can stay here—'

' It doesn't. It's just another reason why we should find somewhere else quickly.'

' If we do that, it'll bring all our creditors down on us. We've got to keep up appearances, Sara. Anyway, if you'd only see reason we wouldn't need to worry. If the people we owe money to knew we were selling out, they'd be content to wait.'

Sara stared at her, surprised to find her so knowledgeable, so determined to sacrifice the business which had been so important to her husband.

' I can't help that, and all Brent's doing is to get us time to pay.'

' Is it? I wouldn't have thought even he would be so mean, with all his money.'

' He isn't, Val. It was me who refused to let him pay, but he has promised to look out for a cheaper flat for us, so we can get rid of this burden.'

' That's big of him, but he needn't bother. I don't want to leave here. I'm surprised at you, Sara. I'd have thought you'd have more pride than to keep running to him for help.'

That was something Sara herself wondered about, because it was completely against her nature. Yet what alternative had she? Everything she had done, no matter how difficult she had found it and how alien to her, had been done for Jamie, so that if he wanted his inheritance it would be there, waiting for him and not sold without reference to him. Though only she knew how much it had cost her to take the steps necessary to ensure that, and Brent had made it possible for her to try. Val had called him mean, but in that moment of truth Sara admitted that she had been wrong.

Whatever Brent Maxwell's faults were, meanness was not among them, and perhaps one day Val, too, might acknowledge that.

The next few days were quiet ones for Sara. When she had gone to the store the day after talking to Brent at the apartment, it was to learn from Céleste that Terry had gone to Paris early that morning.

'To Paris? But he didn't say anything about it yesterday,' she exclaimed.

'Didn't he? It was pretty sudden, I suppose. Of course he knew he'd have to go soon, but he discovered yesterday afternoon that he'd be needed earlier.'

'I see. Thanks for telling me,' Sara said, and settled down again to her work.

Meticulously in the days that followed she checked through the books and, when she needed a rest from that, walked through the store in an effort to become accustomed to the routine and to get to know the staff.

But it was not an easy task, as she said to Mollie when she met her for coffee in the staff dining room.

'I can't make them out. They're so standoffish with me. You'd think they'd be glad one of the family was taking an interest in them and in the store.'

Mollie shook her head.

'They've heard rumours, Sara, and they're worried about the future. I think they'd feel better if there was a new owner with plenty of money to spend.'

'You mean they know there's been an offer? Who told them about it?'

'These things get around,' Mollie said evasively.

'Only because somebody makes it his business to do that, surely?'

'Perhaps.' Mollie looked at her obliquely. 'How are you getting on with your researches? Have you found anything yet?'

'Not really. There are a few things I don't understand, but apart from them—'

'Some of those who used to work here could tell you a few things,' Mollie said suddenly, then covered her mouth with her hands, looking pleadingly at Sara. 'I shouldn't have said that. Forget it! Promise you will.'

Sara shook her head.

'I can't forget it, but I won't tell anyone what you've said, Mollie.' She sighed. 'I feel as if there's a conspiracy of silence everywhere. I can't understand it. When we undertake this kind of investigation in the States, everybody tries to help, but here—'

'Here you've got—' Mollie stopped and closed her lips firmly. 'No, I won't say it. My job is too important to me to jeopardise it.'

Sara looked at her earnestly.

' Mollie, believe me, you needn't worry. Nothing you tell me will be held against you. I promise you that.'

' I know you mean it, Sara, but I daren't risk it. I've seen it happen too often. People have been here one day, then gone the next. I've got Mother to think of, not just myself.' She got up and leaned against the table, looking apologetically at Sara. ' Remember that, won't you, and don't think too badly of me.'

Sara watched her walk quickly out of the dining room, then followed more slowly, trying to understand what she had heard.

It seemed clear enough that Mollie knew something of what had been going on, that others had also known and had been dismissed because of that knowledge. Yet how could it have happened while David had been in control?

She was still frowning over the problem when she walked into her office, to stop short in surprise as Brent Maxwell got up from the visitor's chair in front of the desk.

' What are you doing here?' she asked.

' I called to tell you I've found a flat. Can you come and look at it?'

' Now? But—'

' Yes, while I've got the key.'

' But I've so much to do.'

He sighed.

' As if that matters! It can wait, surely, for an hour or so. I thought a cheaper flat was important to you.'

She glared at him, this man who always had to have his own way, who rode roughshod over everyone's feelings, especially hers. Though she doubted if it ever occurred to him that anyone had feelings which might be hurt.

' That's where you're wrong. I'm just at a crucial point. It's too bad you've made these arrangements. Perhaps next time you'll find out first if it's convenient.'

She could hear her voice rising and clamped her lips together, trying to hold on to her control.

' Now what's wrong?' he asked in a long-suffering voice, and she felt a choking sensation in her throat and knew that in spite of all her efforts she was not going to be able to do it.

She took a deep calming breath, clenching her hands tightly together, preparatory to telling him exactly what she thought of him, but before she could say anything, he added,

' If you're not the most contrary girl I've ever known! I did try to telephone you, or at least my secretary did, but although you're so busy, you weren't in your office and no one seemed to know where you were. You seem to have forgotten you asked me to do what I could to help you. However, if you've changed your mind, please tell me. That's all you need to do, you know. Then I won't bother you any more.'

She did not look directly at him, her innate sense of fair play telling her that every word he said was the truth. Not that this endeared him to her in the least. On the contrary, it only increased her dislike of him, especially as she knew she could not do as he suggested. That it was impossible for her to look him straight in the eye and tell him to go away, that she was quite capable of dealing with everything herself.

She did not have enough time for that. This man had given her three months to get the finances of the store in some sort of order. If she was to succeed at all, she needed every moment she could snatch, so how could she at the same time look for an apartment?

She swallowed hard, knowing she must accept his help no matter how much she hated to do so, and said coldly,

'I'm sorry. Of course I'll come and look over the apartment now. It's most kind of you to take all this trouble for us.'

'Kind!' he mocked. 'You've suddenly found your party manners, haven't you? I'm not sure I like them, Sara.'

'Then you'll have to lump them,' she flashed. 'It's evident that nothing I can do will ever suit you, so you'll just have to put up with it.'

' That's better! I was beginning to think you were sickening for something. No, pax!' he laughed as her eyes flashed fire at him. ' I take it all back. Come and look at the flat before you make up your mind that nothing I recommend will suit you!'

This was so near to the truth that she found herself quite unable to answer, and when he put his hand under her elbow, went with him quite meekly down the stairs and out of the shop.

He stopped at a low sports car parked nearby and opened the door for her.

' Jump in. It's not far away, but we may as well drive there.'

She got in without answering and was surprised, in spite of what he had said, when after a very few minutes he stopped in a narrow street of high terraced houses.

She looked at them, her heart sinking, her thoughts very obviously mirrored in her expressive face.

' Don't look like that,' he said. ' The outside may not be wonderful, but I think you'll find the inside very much more to your taste.'

She did not really believe him but allowed him to lead her up the steps of the house. Brent opened the front door with the key and stood aside to allow her to go in.

Sara did so, then stopped in astonishment, looking around her and seeing a spacious hall with a beautiful curving staircase to the upper floor, bright and shining with yellow paint which made it look as if the hall was full of sunbeams.

'This hall was once the ground floor of two houses. The whole row has been converted into flats and the front ground floor one on this side is empty.'

He inserted a key in the door and pushed it open. Sara went hesitantly inside, finding herself in a narrow lobby with doors leading off it. He opened them in turn.

'This is the sitting room and next to it is a good sized kitchen with a dining alcove. Then there's the bathroom with a shower and three bedrooms.'

Sara followed him from room to room, admitting, though not yet willingly, that he had been right. It was the ideal apartment for them. Spacious, with high ceilings, light and airy, the big windows catching the sunshine, the central heating unobtrusive, the decorations fresh and bright, the furnishings good.

'Well?' he asked when she did not speak. 'Will it do?'

'Yes,' she said, and then was annoyed with herself for the brevity of her answer.

Because she disliked him and thought him autocratic and too often right, was no excuse for her being bad-mannered and ungrateful.

'You were quite right, Brent.' She spoke quickly and gratefully. 'It's exactly the kind of apartment we need. Thank you for finding it.'

'You think Val will like it, too?'

'She'll have to,' Sara answered with decision. 'She can't stay where she is and—' She looked at him as a worrying idea occurred to her. 'If we can afford it. Is it very expensive?'

'No, quite reasonable for a furnished flat.' He named an amount which to her, accustomed to the high rents of American apartments and compared with that charged for the purpose-built one Val and David had occupied, seemed ridiculously cheap.

'Are you sure?' she asked, putting her doubt into words. 'You haven't made a mistake?'

'Of course not. Can you afford it?'

'Oh, yes. Thanks again, Brent, I'm sorry if I seemed ungrateful, but—'

'I know exactly how you felt,' he said, and the hot colour flooded into her cheeks at the implied rebuke, which she knew was well deserved. 'If you're really sure, then we may as well go along and clinch the deal. Unless you want Val to see it first?'

'No. She must accept my word that it's suitable,' Sara said with decision.

His deep blue eyes crinkled into laughter.

' I knew you for an autocrat the moment I saw you! Come along, then, and we'll get everything fixed up.'

The hot colour was still burning in her cheeks as she went with him to his car again. It was not until she was seated in the agent's office and was signing the lease he produced that she recovered her usual spirit in some measure.

' You're sure the rent is correct?' she asked, her pen poised over the document.

The agent smiled, flicking a glance at Brent.

' Yes, quite right. It's as agreed, isn't it, Mr Maxwell?'

' Exactly as agreed.' He looked at his watch. ' There's just time for us to have lunch, Sara, before I go on to another appointment. I know just the place where we'll be served quickly with excellent food. Come along.'

She went with him, not wanting to argue about it in the agent's office, but as soon as they were outside, she said sharply,

' There's no need to think you've got to give me lunch, you know.'

He put his hands on her shoulders and gave her a little shake.

' When will you learn to accept an invitation gracefully, Sara? I want to give you lunch, so come along and don't argue.'

'I wasn't going to—' she began.

'Good. That makes a change. Do one thing for me, will you?'

She looked at him, suspicion in her dark eyes.

'Such as what?'

'Give me the pleasure of your company for an hour or so without trying to fight me every minute of the time.'

She was so taken aback by his words that she got meekly into the car, and had barely recovered from them when they were being ushered to a table in the window of the restaurant he had chosen.

'This is my club,' he said as they sat down. 'You can always be sure of a good meal here, even at short notice.'

The waiter shook out the table napkin and placed it over her knees, then whisked away the card from the centre of the table. It was only then that she realised it spelled one word, 'Reserved'.

She clenched her hands together, understanding at once that he must have taken it for granted, before he had come to the store, that she would lunch with him. But he was already consulting with the wine waiter and she was being handed a menu.

This was no time to have a showdown with him, and anyway she had recklessly promised that she would not fight him while they had lunch, perhaps

85

not so much in words as by tacit acceptance. But as she looked at the menu she vowed to herself that one day, before very long, she would teach this man a lesson.

She would make it clear to him that she would not tolerate his arrogant ways, though she did not specify how she was going to do it.

CHAPTER VII

The lunch was all that Brent had said it would be, and as she went into her office later, Sara admitted to herself that nobody could have been a more charming companion during that hour of truce which he had asked for and which she had so grudgingly given.

Looking back, she could hardly believe she had been with the same man. Then she smiled at herself wryly. Just because he had shown so much interest in her work with Johnnie in America and had asked so many intelligent questions, she was imagining that this particular leopard had changed his spots.

Of course he had not, she told herself sharply. He had promised her an excellent lunch in congenial company and it was in keeping with his character that he had so meticulously carried out what he had promised.

Though in spite of that thought, as she pulled the ledger towards her and picked up her pencil, she was aware of a warm feeling of comfort within her.

Because in spite of his so annoying assumption of omnipotence he had proved one thing, that he had remembered about her and her problems and had acted at once to produce the ideal answer to them. And for that she must always be grateful to him.

Though she did not know why he had done so, and though she thought about it for a long time, she could find no answer to the mystery. It was not easy to forget about it and concentrate on the work she had to do, but she made a determined effort.

After a while the familiar task engrossed her completely as she searched for the answer to the question which had troubled her for days, the question of what had happened to the money from the sale of her brother's home.

She had just convinced herself that there was no entry to cover it when the door opened and Terry came in.

She looked up with a start, dragging her mind back to the present.

' Hi, Sara,' he said. ' How are things going?'

' All right. Why did you go to Paris? It was a very sudden decision, wasn't it?'

' Not really. I knew I'd have to go sooner or later to try to pick up the threads. It just happened to become necessary earlier than I expected, that's all. I came in before to ask you to have lunch with me again, but you were out.'

' Yes. Brent Maxwell called and I lunched with him.'

He raised his eyebrows.

'Did you? That's a surprise.'

'Why should it be?'

'Well, after his display of temper in the store, I'd have thought you'd never have spoken to him again.'

He spoke lightly enough, but Sara could sense a sharpness under the words which was at variance with his off-hand attitude, and she asked probingly,

'Did you expect that to happen?'

He laughed shortly.

'Oh, come now, Sara, that's putting a meaning into what I said that wasn't intended. Although knowing you, I must say it wouldn't have surprised me in the slightest if you had quarrelled permanently with him after the way he spoke to you. In front of the staff, too.'

'I might have done,' she agreed, 'if he hadn't come to see me later, to apologise.'

'Maxwell apologised? I don't believe it.'

'It's true, though. He realised afterwards that I knew nothing about the phone call. Who do you think made it, Terry?'

'How should I know? Perhaps he dreamed the whole thing up.'

'Why on earth should he do that?'

He shrugged.

'Who knows what his motives may be? For instance, why should he call and take you out to lunch today?'

She was unreasonably irritated by his words.

'What do you mean by that?'

'Oh, I didn't mean to suggest he took you out for any other reason than to sit and look at you, my lovely Sara. I wouldn't be so uncomplimentary.'

'Don't be ridiculous. If you must know, he's found a cheaper flat for us and he took me to look over it.'

'That was quick work, but then he's got a lot of irons in the fire.'

'You mean it'd be one of his flats?'

He lifted his hands expressively.

'Who knows? But I can tell you one thing, you haven't got his measure yet, Sara.'

'Perhaps not, but at least I can be grateful for the trouble he's taken,' she said with asperity.

'Oh, certainly.' He came round the desk and looked at the columns of figures she had written down. 'How are you getting on? Have you found anything yet?'

'It's what I can't find that's worrying me. Do you think David used the money from the sale of the house to pay off mortgages?'

He moved away from her and she sensed a moment's indecision as if he was making up his mind what to say. Though when he did answer his voice was confident enough.

'Definitely not,' he answered smoothly. 'He thought at first that he might raise a mortgage, but he found he could get a lot more money by selling, so he did.'

'Then what can have happened to it?'

'I've told you that already.'

She looked at him, her dark eyes bright with annoyance, resenting the implication behind his words with a depth of feeling which surprised her.

'I know you have, and I don't believe it. I asked Brent if he'd had the money and he said he hadn't.'

Terry sat down on the corner of the desk.

'Of course he did, my dear. He's hardly likely to admit it, is he?'

'I believe him, Terry.'

'Which means that you don't believe me? I'm hurt, Sara.'

She made an impatient movement.

'I don't mean it like that at all——'

'Don't you?' He got up and went towards the door, turning when he reached it, his hand on the knob. 'Are you sure?' he asked, and in one movement opened the door and went out.

She sat and stared in front of her, acknowledging that he had some grounds for the reproach in his voice. Because what he said was true. She did believe Brent Maxwell and, having acknowledged that, it followed that she did not believe Terry. How could she when she definitely suspected him of deliberately misleading her about so many things?

She sighed, pushing the honey gold hair back from her hot forehead. Never had she felt so confused about anything as she did at that moment. She who had always prided herself on the clarity of her mind, whom Johnnie had always called his ' clear-thinking ' girl.

Her mouth twisted wryly. He would certainly change his ideas if he could only see the turmoil in her brain now!

She pulled the stock ledger towards her, determined that she would concentrate on one of the most obvious sources of loss in a business and forget about the so exasperating Brent Maxwell, and before long she was immersed in the work to the exclusion of everything else.

Because a very definite picture began to emerge as she checked the purchase of materials against the entries in the stores ledger, finding again and again that expensive consignments of cloth of all kinds were not entered. Carefully she noted down the discrepancies, then took one item, an outrageously dear gold embroidered silk, and checked through the whole ledger, looking for an entry. There was nothing at all to be found, and she sat back in her chair, looking frowningly in front of her, wondering who she should approach first about it. Then her brow cleared.

How stupid of her! Of course, Mollie was in charge of stores. She would know, if anyone did, what had happened to the missing stock.

She pulled the internal telephone towards her and dialled the stock room number and when Mollie's voice answered her, said crisply,

'Sara here. Can you spare the time to come to my office, Mollie?'

'Yes. In about ten minutes, if that's all right.'

'Yes, fine. See you then.'

Sara cradled the receiver, trying to work out the best way in which to approach this woman whom she had known so long. By the time Mollie came, she had made up her mind. Only the plain truth would serve. That would be the way Mollie would prefer it, she was sure.

'Sorry to keep you waiting,' Mollie apologised as she came in.

'That's all right. I want you to help me, if you can. Come and look at this item, bought about four months ago. Have you any idea what happened to it?'

Mollie looked down at the entry in the purchase ledger and shook her head.

'I don't remember it, but the stores ledger will tell you what happened to it.'

'But it doesn't,' Sara said quietly.

Mollie's forehead creased into worried lines.

'Are you sure?'

93

'Yes, and it's not the only one. Quite a number of very expensive items are missing. Could they have gone straight out to the departments, do you think?'

Mollie shook her head decisively.

'No. Everything should go into stores first, especially the expensive materials. They're only used for the model clothes and wouldn't be issued until they were required. I can't understand it.' She stopped, her usually ruddy cheeks whitening. 'They're my responsibility, but I've never seen them. Honestly, Sara. You've got to believe me.'

Sara put out her hand and touched Mollie's arm gently.

'Of course I believe you, Mollie. Only—what can have happened to them, do you think?'

'I don't know. There are a lot of queer things going on, only I can't talk about them, Sara. You see, those who talked lost their jobs, and I daren't lose mine. My mother's very old and frail now and dependent on me—'

'Don't worry, Mollie. I'll see you're all right, you know that.'

'But you won't always be here.'

Sara was silent for a moment, acknowledging the truth of what Mollie had said.

'Think about it, anyway,' she said at last. 'I won't force you to tell me anything you don't want to.'

'Thanks, Sara. I'll have to go now. People will be wanting me, and if they find me here with you—'

Sara sat quite still after Mollie had gone, hurrying out of the room on the heels of her words, thinking deeply, feeling shocked and worried by what she had heard.

In her father's time old employees particularly had been looked after and valued. Now it seemed they were dismissed if they knew too much and were not afraid to speak up about things which they thought were wrong. She could hardly believe it was true, yet the fact remained that of the people she had known practically all her life, only Mollie was left.

She had not blamed anybody for what had happened, but Sara knew with a slightly sick feeling that the fault must lie with David, who had apparently not cared about the old employees.

The first closing bell, shrilling through the building, roused her from her unhappy thoughts with a jolt, and she quickly gathered the books together and pushed them into a cupboard.

She had intended to go home earlier, to tell Val about the new apartment and break the news that they would be leaving the old one within a week or so, news which she knew would not be at all acceptable to her sister-in-law. And she was right.

'You mean we'll have to go next week? But

95

that's ridiculous! It'll take weeks to sort everything out. And I haven't seen the flat yet. What's all the hurry, Sara?'

'Brent Maxwell's arranged it that way, to save us money. The new apartment's much cheaper than this one. I don't know how he managed to get the agents to give us time to pay, but he must have guaranteed us himself in some way.'

'And why not? He's got plenty of money. David always said he was rolling in wealth.'

'That isn't the point—'

'Nonsense. It wouldn't hurt him to be responsible for a few more pounds. I won't go to some poky little place all in a rush—'

'It isn't poky.' Sara heard her voice rising with irritation and tried to take a hold on her temper. 'It's quite big. You'll like it, Val.'

'Is it like this one?'

'Well, no. It's—'

'There you are, then! I tell you, I won't go there.'

Sara sighed.

'You've no option, Val. Don't you understand, we can't stay here because we can't pay the high rent. It's no use crying,' she added quickly as the easy tears began to stream down Val's cheeks. 'That solves nothing.'

'You're absolutely heartless, Sara. And what about Jamie? It's his half term next week-end and he won't have anywhere to go.'

'I didn't know that, but I can't see that it matters. He can help us to move if he's home in time. If not, he'll come to the new flat instead of the old one, that's all.'

'Poor boy! To lose his father and now to have no proper home either. I don't understand you, Sara. Living in the States has changed you. You're not the same girl I used to know.'

With an effort Sara controlled the stinging reply she would have liked to make, acknowledging that Val had suffered more than one severe shock in the past few weeks which would make this new upheaval even more difficult to accept.

'I'm sorry, Val,' she said instead. 'I've not really changed, you know. It's just that as things are, we can't go on living as we have been. Jamie's a sensible boy. He'll understand.'

Val twisted her handkerchief between her fingers.

'I hope you're right. Oh, why did David have to die like that and cause me all this trouble?'

Sara put a comforting arm around her.

'I don't know, love, but stop worrying. Everything will come right one of these days.'

'I hope so.' Val looked forlornly at Sara. 'It doesn't seem possible that it will. I think I'll go and lie down.'

'Yes, do that, and I'll bring you a cup of tea and

some aspirin to help you to sleep.'

Sara watched her sister-in-law trail lethargically into her bedroom before going into the kitchen to plug in the kettle, a worried frown between her eyes.

If only Val would try to accept that everything must change, but it was probably too much to expect of her. Perhaps when Jamie came home she would feel better because he, Sara was sure, would take any changes in his stride, if he was still the placid boy she remembered. Then he had always been too occupied with his own interests to bother about external things. All he had needed was a roof over his head and plenty of food at regular intervals. And she saw no reason to doubt that he was still the same, if his letters to her were any indication.

No, it was not the thought of Jamie which brought that worried frown to her forehead, a frown that was still there when she took the tray of tea in to Valerie.

CHAPTER VIII

Contrary to Sara's expectations, Val made no more protests about leaving the flat, and over the next few days seemed to recover from her almost hysterical opposition to the plan, although she steadfastly refused to go and see the new apartment.

Sara was glad that at home everything seemed to be comparatively peaceful, because as her investigations at the store proceeded, she was becoming more and more worried.

Always when she walked through, all departments appeared to be very busy, yet although the floor managers assured her that there was a marked increase in trading, cash receipts were considerably down on the previous year. Doggedly she checked and cross-checked, working out costs against receipts, and all the while her concern for the future deepened, as the first of the three months allowed her inexorably ticked away.

Perhaps things might not have seemed so dismal if she had had somebody to share her difficulties, as she had done with Johnnie. But at the store there was always the suspicion that the people who might have helped her could be concerned in the discrepancies, and she did not feel she could approach them.

She was so very much alone in this difficult task she had undertaken so lightly. Days had gone by since Brent had smiled at her and said, ' Au revoir, Sara. See you soon,' but he had not come near. And, strangely enough, it was this which caused her the most concern, as though she had lost something of value to her.

Which was ridiculous, as she told herself fiercely. Three weeks earlier she had not known of his existence, and from the first he had annoyed her by his arrogance and impatience. Yet in spite of it all, she could not help feeling deserted, as if he had abandoned her when she most needed help.

She looked up as the door opened, her pulses leaping hopefully, but it was Terry who came in, and the depression clamped down again.

' Still busy, Sara? How are things working out?' he asked.

' It's too early to be sure yet,' she answered evasively, reluctant to talk to him about her suspicions. There would be time enough for that when she was sure about what had been taking place. ' These things can't be hurried.'

' I suppose not, but if there's anything I can do to help, you've only to ask me.'

' Thanks, Terry, I'll remember that. Oh, by the way, we'll be moving into the new apartment next week and I'll have to take a couple of days off. Will it be all right if I keep the ledgers in here until I'm back again?'

He frowned.

'It's not terribly convenient, Sara, because there's work to be done on them. If you're not using them I'd rather they went back to the office.'

'Just as you like. I don't want to make things difficult for you.'

'You won't do that, I know. If you'll tell me the date you're moving, I'll have them picked up then and brought back when you return.'

'I don't know it yet.'

'Don't you? I thought from the way you spoke that you'd got it all fixed up.'

She hesitated, then said quietly,

'Brent was to let me know when he'd arranged it, but I haven't heard from him yet.'

'Was he? He's being very busy on your behalf. Still, it's not surprising that he hasn't let you know. I heard he'd gone away. He often does for a week or so. He says it's business, but we think he goes to see a rather special girl-friend.'

He laughed, though the eyes which watched Sara so closely did not change their expression.

'It would be very odd if he'd got to his age without having a girl-friend,' she replied, and was relieved to see the suspicion leave his eyes. 'I ought to have made the arrangements myself. It's entirely my own fault.'

'Well, take as much time as you need, my dear.

How does Val like the new flat?'

'She hasn't seen it. She says she won't go near it until she's forced to.'

Terry shook his head.

'You should have left her where she was happy, Sara. Poor Val! Bad enough to lose David without having all her life disrupted as well.'

Sara's eyes flashed in sudden anger.

'That's the silliest thing I've heard you say yet! You of all people know how we're placed. Val has no income from the store and the proceeds from David's life assurance will have to be used to pay off his bank overdraft. She doesn't want to understand, but you should. She's destitute, and you know it.'

'All right, I know it,' he said sharply. 'I also know it's your fault, Sara, because you won't accept the offer that's been made for the business. It's still open, by the way,' he added.

'That only solves things in the short term, Terry,' she said wearily. 'What I'm trying to do is make Val's and Jamie's future secure.'

'And Sara Blake's, too, I think.'

'Perhaps, but if I'm all right, so are they. Don't forget that, Terry.'

'I won't.' He smiled suddenly, making a complete *volte-face*. 'That's quite true, Sara. I admire you for sticking to your guns and you know I'll help you in any way I can.'

' Thank you.'

He turned to go, then came back again and said,

' Oh, you'll be glad to know that we think we've found a designer—a young woman who's been in Paris for the past two years and seems to be on her toes and have plenty of bright ideas.'

' Good.   I'm glad.   When's she coming?'

' As soon as she's released by her present firm. It's a relief to have found somebody so quickly. We could certainly do with a boost, that's for sure.'

She looked at him quickly.

' Is trade as bad as it seems, Terry?   I know takings are down on last year, but the store seems to be very busy.'

He shrugged.

' Plenty of people walking round, but not many buying.'

' I wouldn't have said that, and Mollie tells me the model gown department and the sewing rooms are fantastically busy.'

He frowned.

' Does she?   That shows all she knows about it. There may be a lot of orders in, but costs have risen so steeply over the past few months that we'll be lucky if we make a profit in those departments.'

' You'll have to increase prices, won't you?'

' Yes, as soon as we can.   New models will help, and that's what I hope we'll get as soon as this new girl comes.   Wish me luck, Sara.'

' I do, of course.'

' Thanks. See you,' and before she knew it, he bent and kissed her firmly, then was gone.

Sara sat where he had left her, automatically trying to rub from her lips the impression of the kiss he had left there, feeling unreasonably angry at his action. And yet it was not the first time in her life that Terry had kissed her, only now she did not want his kisses. Judas kisses, she told herself sadly, because she was becoming more and more sure that Terry was behind all the troubles that had overtaken Blake's store.

If only she did not feel so alone! Even Brent Maxwell, irritating as he was with his firm conviction that he was always right, would have been welcome because he at least, whatever his own opinions were, was actively supporting her in her effort to pull the business round.

But he was off on his own concerns, visiting his girl-friend instead of making the arrangements he had promised he would. He was as unreliable as everyone else. One day, she told herself sadly, she would learn her lesson—that nothing was done which she did not do herself; that all her endeavours to do the best she could for them all would be resented and misunderstood.

Only somehow she had thought Brent Maxwell was different. That he understood and sympathised with her. Well, she had been wrong.

Tomorrow she would make her own arrangements, and tonight, as soon as she had eaten her evening meal, she would begin to pack in readiness for the move. And perhaps she might find that Val could be persuaded to help her.

But when she reached home the apartment was empty. There was no note from Val to say where she had gone, though Sara was glad that her sister-in-law, who had spent the past few days alternately in bed or lying on the sofa looking pathetically sorry for herself, had actually roused herself sufficiently to go out.

That must be a good sign, she thought optimistically, as she prepared and ate a scratch meal, because it must mean that Val was beginning to accept the situation with a good grace.

After she had eaten she changed into slacks and tunic, then turned on the record player before beginning to take the books off the shelves in David's study and stack them ready to be packed. But she had hardly begun when the door bell rang.

She went to answer it, wondering who could be calling at that time of night, then stood staring at the last person she had expected to see.

'Good evening, Sara,' Brent Maxwell said. 'Aren't you going to ask me in?'

'What do you want?' she demanded.

'To see you, of course. What else?'

'That's very good of you, but as you've managed

to live so many days without getting in touch with me, I don't think it matters—'

' Now what are you talking about?' He pushed the door wide open and stepped into the hall, and she backed in front of him.

' I wasn't aware that I'd asked you to come in,' she said militantly.

' I know you didn't, but I thought you'd probably just forgotten your manners.' He looked down at her with the sudden unexpected smile that lit up his eyes so magically. ' Aren't you glad to see me, Sara?'

' Only so that I can tell you what I think of you for not doing what you promised. Though, naturally, I can hardly expect you to give up your pleasures for me.'

' Certainly not.' He walked past her, taking her arm in his hand and leading her inexorably into the sitting room. ' Suppose we sit down comfortably while you tell me about these pleasures I haven't given up.'

She shrugged her arm away from his hand but did not sit down as he suggested. Instead she walked across to the record player and turned it off.

' It's no business of mine,' she said coldly, ' what you do. You're perfectly at liberty to visit your girl-friend if you want to, only I think you might have—'

' Certainly I am,' he interrupted. ' How did you

know where I'd gone?'

'Terry told me,' she said, trying not to let him irritate her into losing her temper, though the rather strange attitude he was adopting was making it difficult for her to achieve.

'Did he? He's very knowledgeable about my affairs.'

'Oh, stop fencing with me! It's nothing to me who you go and see, but—'

He moved suddenly, looking down at her with a half smile, taking her shoulders in his hands. She could feel them burning through the thin silk of her tunic and was acutely aware of his nearness, feeling the pulse in her throat begin to beat strongly.

She saw as if through a mist the deep blue eyes smiling at her and felt a surge of emotion burn through her, so that only the greatest strength of will prevented her from swaying towards him, to lose herself in those bright, hypnotic eyes.

She gasped and pulled away from him, breaking his hold on her, and moved over to the window, trying to control the wild beating of her heart, to hide from him the agitation his nearness had raised in her.

What was the matter with her? Why should he, whom she did not even like, who annoyed her by his arbitrary, arrogant treatment of her, affect her like this? As though she had drunk heady champagne and all the joy bells in the world were ringing?

Thankfully she realised that he had not moved and after a moment she was able to turn towards him and say in a casual voice that pleased her,

'What did you come for?'

He did not answer immediately but stood looking down, the deep lines of his face very much in evidence.

'To see if the arrangements I've made were suitable,' he said at last.

'What arrangements?'

He looked at her then in surprise.

'Didn't Jane, my secretary, ring you?'

'No. Should she have done?'

'Yes. I was called away suddenly—not to visit my girl-friend, as you apparently thought, but to go to my grandmother who is very dear to me. I asked Jane to telephone the arrangements I'd made to you. You're sure she didn't?'

'Well, honestly! I'm not quite out of my mind yet. Of course she didn't,' Sara said indignantly.

'I'm sorry, but it's not like Jane to forget anything.'

'She's slipped up this time. You didn't mention it to her when you got back?'

'I haven't seen her yet. I only arrived about an hour ago and I came straight here. I thought you'd be expecting me.'

She was disarmed by his answer and ashamed of herself because she had misjudged him so badly. Though underneath she was aware of a warm feeling of comfort for which she could find no reason, except the relief of knowing that after all he had not neglected her for some mythical girl-friend.

'What arrangements have you made?' she asked at last.

He told her, adding anxiously,

'It's very short notice now, Sara, for the day after tomorrow. Can you manage it, do you think?'

'I'll have to. I've started to stack all the books and maybe I'll finish them tonight. Then—'

'I hoped you'd come and have a meal with me.'

She was conscious again of the breathlessness which had seized her earlier, and it was an effort to say calmly,

'Now? Tonight? I'm afraid I can't. There's so much to do if I'm to be ready in time.'

'Leave it,' he said masterfully. 'My men will do everything for you, if you'll direct them.'

She hesitated.

'If that's all right—it would certainly save me a lot of work,' she said slowly.

'I wouldn't offer if it wasn't. You'll come, then?'

'Yes. Thank you. If you'll give me a few minutes to change—'

'As long as you like, Sara. Take your time.'

But she did not keep him waiting long, coming in to him in less than twenty minutes wearing one of her favourite outfits, a blue green dress of wild silk with a neckline trimming of thick embroidery interspersed with sparkling beads which caught the light as she moved, covered by a loose matching coat. It had been a real extravagance when she had bought it, but now she was glad, wanting in some obscure way to look her very best while she was out with this man.

'You look very lovely, Sara,' he said when she came in. 'That's a gorgeous colour and it suits you.'

She felt the pleased colour deepen in her cheeks.

'Thank you. I'm glad you approve,' she said provocatively. 'I think we make a handsome couple, don't you?'

He laughed.

'Though unlike the birds, where it's the male who wears the brilliant feathers while the female looks pretty drab!'

That laughing remark seemed to set the tone for the rest of the evening. Brent took her to a quiet but elegant restaurant with tables set in alcoves, where the food was excellent and the service unobtrusive and efficient, and for the remainder of the evening Sara forgot all the troubles which had been piling on to her during the past weeks.

The time passed very quickly and happily and Sara was very sorry when the time came to go back home. Brent drove her to the block of apartments and went with her to the lift doors.

He pressed the button, then as they waited took her hands in his, smiling at her in a way that made her legs feel as if all the bones had been removed from them.

'Thank you for a perfect evening, Sara,' he said as the lift doors opened silently behind her. 'I won't come up to the flat with you in case Val is there, but I'll see you tomorrow.'

'Tomorrow?' she repeated in surprise.

'Yes. It's nearly one o'clock in the morning. Sleep well, Sara. Take care of yourself.'

He bent his head and she felt his lips against hers for a brief moment, then he was gone, striding across the foyer to the front doors. She waited until he reached them, and raised an unsteady hand in farewell as he turned to look back at her before going out.

Then she went into the lift and was carried up to the apartment, aware only of the turbulent emotions which surged through her, making her feel weak and breathless.

What was there about this man that he should have such an effect on her? Certainly she had spent an enjoyable evening with him, but that did not alter the fact that their characters were totally at variance. Yet Johnnie, whom she was so fond of, had never raised such feelings in her when he had kissed her, had never made her think she was floating on a golden cloud of joyous happiness.

'You'll have to. For one thing, this is a party line, and you
know what that means. For another, as it's taken only ten
days for a garbled version to reach your mother, how long

CHAPTER IX

The apartment was in darkness when Sara let herself in, and she went quietly into the sitting room
so that she would not disturb Val, and switched on
a table lamp. She sat down in the nearest chair,
feeling drained of all strength, glad that there was
nobody about to see how disturbed she was.

Then she heard Val's voice calling to her from
her bedroom and got up quickly, going to the door
to answer in case her sister-in-law got up and came
in to her.

'What is it, Val? What's wrong?'

'Nothing. I wondered what had happened to
you. You're very late. Where've you been?'

'I might ask you the same question.'

'I came in ages ago. I've been in bed for hours.
Come and talk to me, Sara. There's no point in
standing in the hall.'

'All right.' Reluctantly she crossed to Val's
room and went in, glad to find she had switched
on a rose-shaded bedside lamp which shed a low,
diffused light across the bed, leaving the remainder
of the room in semi-darkness. Val's eyes were too
sharp to risk being seen by her in a bright light,
Sara thought, as she walked across to the dressing
table and sat down on the stool in front of it. 'I

tried not to wake you, Val. I've been out to dinner with Brent Maxwell.'

'That man? Poor you!'

'I had a very pleasant time. Where did you go, Val?'

'Terry rang me and asked me to have a meal with him, so I thought I might as well go,' she said defensively.

'Why not? You've got to start going out sometime. Did you enjoy it?'

'Yes, thoroughly. It's such ages since I went anywhere. Oh, by the way, I've heard from Jamie. He's coming home at the week-end.'

'Oh, good. We'll have to meet him at the station. We'll be in the new apartment by then.'

Val sat up quickly.

'In the new apartment? What do you mean?'

'We're moving tomorrow. Brent arranged it and asked his secretary to let us know, but she must have forgotten. But it doesn't really matter. He says his men will see to everything for us, so there's no harm done.'

'That's a matter of opinion! How dare you make all these arrangements without consulting me? You take too much on yourself, Sara!'

'I'm sorry, Val. It's just unfortunate that we weren't told earlier, but we knew we'd got to move quickly and once we'd found somewhere to live—'

'Once you found it, you mean. My wishes

weren't regarded, that's for sure.'

Sara sighed, feeling too tired to go on arguing with her sister-in-law, all the happiness she had been filled with gone as if it had never been.

'You know we've no alternative, Val. Anyway, it's all arranged now and there's nothing to be done about it.'

Val's lips thinned and her face looked suddenly sharp and pinched, no longer sweetly pretty.

'If you'd done as Terry wanted you to, none of this need have happened.'

'Don't start that again, Val,' Sara answered wearily. 'I know Terry's convinced you that if we'd sold the business everything would have been all right, but I know it wouldn't. I did what seemed right for us all.'

'Well, I don't think it was. I'm sure Terry knows more about the store than you do.'

'Perhaps he does, but it's too late to change our plans now. This apartment has been given up and we've got to go.'

Val hunched her smooth shoulders pettishly.

'I'll be out all that day, so don't expect me to do anything to help.'

'I won't. Brent's men will see to everything. You'll only have to get into a taxi when you're ready and drive across to the new place.'

'It sounds to me as if that man's got far too much influence over you,' Val said sharply. 'Why don't you think for yourself for a change? Can't you see he's got his own axe to grind?'

Sara took a deep calming breath.

'No, I can't, and I don't agree that I'm influenced by Brent Maxwell. I don't even like him. Anyway, I'm too tired to argue with you, Val. I'm going to bed.'

'Suit yourself,' Val said, and switched off the light, leaving Sara to grope her way in darkness to her own room. But it was a long time before she went to sleep. Whether it was because of the emotional upheaval she had experienced earlier that night or her final clash with Val, she could not rest, and the dawn was breaking before she finally fell asleep.

It was late when she woke and she was annoyed with herself for wasting time which was so valuable to her. Because although Brent had said to leave it all to him, she knew she could not do that. Everything would have to be sorted out carefully before it could be packed for removal.

She rang Terry as soon as she got up to tell him she would not be in for a while, then began the task of clearing out wardrobes, cupboards and chests, sorting and dusting the books in David's study, gathering the household linen together and collecting all the china and crockery into one place.

As she had promised, Val did nothing at all to help, but spent the day in her bedroom, only coming out to eat the meals which Sara got ready.

She was worn out by the time evening came and went early to bed. She fell at once into a deep sleep from which she awoke next morning feeling much more rested but not looking forward to the day which stretched before her.

Long before Brent came with his workmen to begin to pack everything into the cases they had brought, Val had gone out.

When Sara told him Brent said nothing, but smiled rather grimly, and when she began to help the workmen said peremptorily,

'There's no need for you to do anything. You can leave it all to us.'

'I suppose you'll allow me to make some tea or coffee for you?' she asked with deceptive sweetness.

He smiled, not deceived by her tone.

'Sorry! There I go again, saying the wrong thing. You've done enough, Sara. It doesn't need much intelligence to know you must have spent the whole of yesterday clearing up. But we'll be grateful if you would make us some tea. Thank you.'

'I simply can't win!' Sara thought as she went into the kitchen and plugged in the coffee percolator and the electric kettle. Was Val right in what she said? Was she allowing Brent Maxwell to assume too much importance in her life, letting him rule her and think for her?

Then she shrugged off the suspicion. It was easy for Val to tell her she should not accept the help Brent had given her so willingly. If she did not, then who was there in the whole wide world whom she could rely on?

She was right to accept with gratitude, in spite of anything Val might say. Once today was over she would have little or no contact with him, apart from a limited and purely business one.

Though she did not know at that moment just how wrong she was soon going to be proved.

Brent and his men worked quickly and well so that by the time the removal van came everything was ready. He came into the kitchen where Sara was putting the crockery they had used into her basket and said,

'That's the lot, Sara. My foreman will stay and see everything out. Are you ready to go now?'

'Yes. Oughtn't we to check everything? There's a repair clause in the lease, isn't there?'

'So I believe. I've looked around and made a few notes. The agents are bound to find something which needs doing—but we can come to an agreement about that later. There's no need for you to worry about it.'

'But there is. You've done enough for us, Brent. I can't let you do any more. I wouldn't ask it of you.'

'I wasn't aware that you had,' he said brusquely.

' Anything I do is because I want to.'

' But you're doing so much, and we haven't even thanked you properly.'

' I don't want your thanks. Come along, Sara. It's time we were going, otherwise the van will arrive before we do.'

' All right.'

Automatically she picked up her coat and the basket and went with him out of the apartment, wondering what he had meant by the heavy stress on the word ' your ' when he had said ' I don't want your thanks.'

She stole a look at his face as they went down to the foyer, as though she could find the answer to that question in it, but it was dark and expressionless.

He hardly spoke as they drove through the heavy lunchtime traffic and drew up at last behind Brent's van which had preceded them.

' I'll let the men in, Sara, and they can have their lunch here. Then we'll go and have ours and be ready when the removal van arrives.'

' I can't do that. Jamie is coming in at two o'clock and I've got to meet him. He doesn't know the new address. I'm sorry, Brent—'

' Stop panicking, Sara. I thought you were a level-headed person. I'l take you to the station, then we can all go and have lunch together. I've no doubt Jamie will be hungry even if he's had sandwiches on the train, if I know anything about boys.'

' It's very kind of you, Brent. You must be quite tired of us. You're always having to pull us out of some difficulty or another. If it isn't too much trouble——'

' I wouldn't offer if it was,' he said coolly. ' Come along then, or the train will be in before we get there.'

But they arrived just as it was pulling in to the platform and Sara waited with a beating heart, hoping that she would recognise the nephew she had not seen for three years.

She need not have worried about that. She knew him at once, coming through the barrier with his duffle bag over his shoulder, looking so like David that a stab of pain shot through her.

' Jamie!' she called, and he turned quickly, his face breaking into a wide grin as he recognised her.

' Aunt Sara! Mum said you'd come home. Where is she?'

Sara heard the note of uncertainty in his voice and said gaily,

' She's busy today because we're moving house. That's why we came to meet you. This is Brent Maxwell, Jamie.'

' Hi,' Jamie said, and Brent smiled down at him.

' Had a good journey?'

' Okay. Is Mum at home, then?'

' No, not yet, though she may be by the time we get back. We thought we'd have lunch first, if you feel like it.'

' Rather, I'm famished!'

They had walked towards the car while they were talking and when they stopped beside it, Jamie said admiringly,

' What a super job, Aunt Sara. Is it yours?'

She laughed.

' No such luck! It's Mr Maxwell's.'

Brent smiled.

' Get in and we'll go and have lunch somewhere.'

When they were seated in the restaurant and Jamie was giving a demonstration of his claim to be famished, Sara said diffidently,

' I hope you'll like the new apartment, Jamie. It's not as big as the other one, but—'

' It'll be okay, I suppose. Do I have a room of my own?'

' Oh, yes. I hope you'll like it. The walls are plain white so that you can stick anything you want on them.'

He put down his knife and fork and looked at her eagerly.

' You mean I can put up posters or photos? That'll be great! In the other flat I wasn't allowed to do anything like that in case it spoiled the walls.'

Sara breathed a sigh of relief, knowing that one

hurdle which she had dreaded was past. Now it was only Val whom she had to worry about. She crossed her fingers, hoping she would not delay too long in coming to the new apartment, for Jamie's sake. Because she knew that although Jamie was presenting a happy-go-lucky picture to the world, underneath he was unsure and worried, in case he should lose his mother as suddenly and irrevocably as his father had gone.

They went back to the flat to find the removal van already there, and after that Sara saw very little of Jamie as he helped the men as they tramped in and out of the house.

The next couple of hours were busy ones, but at the end of that time all their furniture was in place and Brent's men were putting up the curtains and unpacking the crates again.

While they were doing that, Sara went quietly round from room to room, already feeling more at home in this new apartment than she had ever done in the old one. Surely even Val would have to admit that she liked its homely and warm atmosphere far better than the modern, almost clinical one they had left?

'Sara!'

She started as Brent called her name and went back into the sitting room.

'I was just looking round—'

'Everything's unpacked, but I'm afraid you'll

have to put most of the stuff away yourself because only you know where it will go. You can have the men to help, if you wish—'

' No, you've done enough, Brent,' she interrupted. ' I'm not sure where to put everything yet. I'll have to do some thinking and planning, and there's no point in keeping them all hanging about. Will you give them this and say how much I appreciate all they've done?'

He made no attempt to take the money she held out to him.

' They don't want that, Sara. They're not expecting it.'

' Nevertheless, please give it to them,' she said quietly. ' I want them to have it.'

He smiled then.

' Oh, very well. I suppose I must let you have your own way over this.'

' It'll be a change if you do,' she could not help saying tartly.

He looked at her in surprise.

' What do you mean by that?'

' What I say. I should think it'll be the very first time you've ever let me do as I want. Mostly you spend your time making sure everybody does exactly as you want.'

He seemed thunderstruck by her accusation.

' I do? I can't imagine what gives you that idea, Sara.'

She laughed.

' I was beginning to suspect you didn't even start to know just how autocratic you are, Brent Maxwell.'

' That accusation from you! Pot calling the kettle black! ' he said.

' Let's not quarrel over who's the worst because we'll never agree. Just let me say how much I appreciate all you've done for us, Brent.'

His eyes smiled down at her.

' If you only knew, Sara—' he said, then stopped as Jamie came bouncing in.

' My room's super, Aunt Sara. Has Mum come yet?'

' Not yet, but she shouldn't be long. Say goodbye to Mr Maxwell. He's going now.'

' Cheerio,' Jamie said. ' I'll come with you to the door. You won't forget what you promised, will you?' Sara heard him say as they went out of the room.

She waited for him to come back and said at once,

' What did Brent promise?'

' To take me over his mill tomorrow. I remember Dad telling me how smashing it was, so I asked him. I've got to write a holiday essay, too, so I can do it about that. If you don't want me for anything, I'll go and put a few things up on my bedroom walls.'

'You do that, Jamie,' Sara said with a smile.

He paused at the door.

'You'll let me know when Mum arrives?'

'Of course. Anyway, you're bound to hear her, you know.'

'Just in case I don't, that's all,' he said in an offhand way which did not deceive Sara, and she wished with all her heart that Val would come quickly, for the boy's sake, and that when she did she would not unsettle him by being openly unhappy about their new home.

Val came earlier than Sara had expected and Jamie, hearing her voice in the hall, came flying out of his room, full of enthusiasm for the new house and anxious to show her what he had already done in his room.

Whether it was her son's obvious happiness or not Sara did not know, but certainly her sister-in-law accepted the move much more gracefully than Sara had expected, and when she left Val and Jamie together in the sitting room and went into the kitchen to prepare the evening meal for them all, she felt more cheerful and lighthearted than she had done since she had come home.

CHAPTER X

Sara was still feeling happy when she went to the store a few mornings later. Val had settled down in the flat quite well and she and Jamie had thoroughly enjoyed their short time together.

It really seemed, Sara thought optimistically, as though everything was beginning to improve for them, that she was right to feel more hopeful about the future. So that the blow she was dealt almost as soon as she arrived in her office was the harder to bear or to accept.

Terry came in just as she was hanging her coat in the cupboard, and she greeted him cheerfully.

' Hello. I hope I didn't stay off too long, Terry, but there was so much to be done and Jamie was on his half-term holiday. How have things been going here?'

' I don't know, Sara. I haven't had time to find out yet.'

She looked at him enquiringly.

' What do you mean?'

He walked over to the window and stood looking out, idly playing with the blind cord.

' I don't know how to tell you this, Sara. The day you moved house I had a letter from Paris, and as a result of that, I went over there the same day.'

'To Paris again? Why, Terry?'

'Because—Sara, something awful has happened.'
Her eyes widened in apprehension.

'What are you talking about?'

'Sit down and I'll tell you.' He waited until she
was seated, but did not follow suit himself, prowl-
ing about the room as he talked. 'This letter was
from somebody who signed herself Yvonne Blake.'

'Yvonne Blake?' Sara echoed.

'Yes. Sara, she said she was David's widow and
wanted to claim his estate on behalf of her three
sons.'
Sara gazed at him in horror.

'I don't believe it! It can't be true!'

'But it is. I thought about it, then I decided
the best thing to do was to go to Paris and see her.
She'd given a telephone number, so when I arrived
I rang her and asked her to come and see me.'

'And did she?'
He nodded.

'Yes. She told me she and David were married
sixteen years ago and have three sons aged fifteen,
twelve and ten.'

'I'll never believe it, Terry,' Sara said obstin-
ately. 'She must be making it up.'
He came over to her and put his hands on her
shoulders.

'I felt that way, too. I told her so, and then she
showed me her marriage certificate and the child-

127

ren's birth certificates. It's true right enough, Sara.'

'But that means—what about Val? And Jamie?'

He lifted his hands helplessly.

'I don't know, but it looks as if this woman has a prior claim.'

Sara stared at him, only slowly assimilating what he had told her.

'You say sixteen years ago? But David wasn't going to Paris then. He wasn't even in the firm. He's only done that for the past eight or nine years.'

'You're forgetting,' Terry answered softly. 'I know he didn't come into the business until after he married Val, but before that he was travelling all over the Continent, buying for resale, to Blake's as well as to other firms up and down the country.'

She was silent, looking down at the shabby desk through eyes which saw nothing at all.

'But that means Val and Jamie—' she began at last, then stopped, unable to put the rest of her thoughts into words.

'I'm afraid so. If what this woman says is really true, and I see no reason now to doubt her, then she and her eldest son inherit. The will definitely states that your father's shares are to be left in trust for David's eldest son. We thought it was Jamie, but now it could be this French boy.'

'I'll never believe it of David.' Her voice was strong now, all the indecision gone from it, and there was a fighting look in her eyes. 'He would never have married Val bigamously, which is what you're saying!'

He shrugged.

'You don't really have any option, Sara. Remember I've seen the proofs. And it alters the whole situation, doesn't it? That is if your real reason for not selling the business was the one you gave—to make sure of Val's and Jamie's future.'

She was wary immediately.

'What do you mean?'

'Yvonne Blake says she's practically destitute. She's anxious to get some money, but she isn't vindictive. Naturally she was horrified to hear about Val, but at our second meeting she said she was sorry for her and Jamie and would like them to share in any proceeds.'

'I see,' Sara said slowly. 'You mean, don't you, that if this woman's claim holds and I still don't agree to sell, Val will get nothing?'

'That's putting it the wrong way round. I'd rather say that if you agree, she won't be left destitute.'

'A distinction without a difference,' she answered drily.

He moved towards the door, turning when he reached it and saying quietly,

'Perhaps, but think about it, Sara. It's a tricky position you're in, isn't it?'

It was certainly a very tricky position, as Sara acknowledged honestly to herself as soon as she was alone, and one which she steadfastly refused to accept.

She had never been very close to her half-brother. He had been grown up before she was born, yet she was quite certain that he would not have done such a thing. He had always been kind and loving to her, and although the difference in their ages had been so great, she had loved him dearly and could not believe that it was in his nature to deceive two women in such a way.

She looked back down the years, remembering his marriage to Val, twelve years earlier, at which she had been the youngest bridesmaid, a proud nine-year-old. Surely he would never have allowed such a wedding to take place—Val in a model gown with a full train, with two other bridesmaids as well as Sara. A big affair which had cost hundreds of pounds and to which everybody who was anybody in their and Val's circle had been invited.

The David she had known would never have consented to such a display if at the time he had already been married and was the father of two sons. Nor would he afterwards have had two more sons, Jamie and this unknown boy.

She clenched her hands into fists, her mind made

up. She would never accept this marriage, not until she had proved it to her own satisfaction— and the only way to do that was to go to France and talk to this woman herself. To meet the children, too, and see if there was any likeness to David about them.

Until she had done that she would make no further move, would not agree to anything. She would tell Terry that and ask him for the woman's address so that she could begin her enquiries.

But the prospect filled her with a sick feeling of dismay, because in spite of her championship of David, she was afraid. Terry's story, supported as it seemed to be by proof, was so final.

Yet she knew that unless she proved it conclusively to herself, she would never be able to accept it as fact. For how could David have hidden such a thing from everybody? From their father, from Val, from the old employees at the store? Surely they would have heard rumours of some kind? If only she had the courage to ask them!

Then she remembered. There were none of the old staff left except Mollie. Her mind flinched away from the implications behind that fact. Was this the reason why no attempt had been made to keep them? Then she pushed that suspicion resolutely from her.

It could not be true, and the easiest way to find out was to see Mollie and ask her, relying on her discretion to make sure that no hint of the story leaked out.

She got up on that decision and went to the stock room, walking through the sewing rooms without seeing any of the workers, her mind fixed on what she was going to say.

She went in without knocking, then stopped in surprise, the words she had been about to speak dying on her lips. Because the person behind the long desk was a complete stranger to her.

She looked up and smiled at Sara, saying chattily,

' Hello. You're Miss Blake, aren't you? I've seen you in the store. Can I get you anything?'

' I'm looking for Mollie Ingham.'

' Mollie?' She left a couple of days ago.'

' Are you sure?'

' I should be. I've been given her job. Céleste said she'd walked out saying she couldn't stand it another minute, and I can't say I blame her. I'm sorry I said I'd take it on. It's too much like hard work.'

' I see,' Sara said slowly. ' Thank you for telling me.'

She was back in her own office before the real meaning of what she had been told occurred to her. Then she heard again Mollie's voice saying to her, ' I can't afford to lose my job. Mother's very old and frail now and she's dependent on me.'

Surely Mollie had never left of her own accord,

132

thrown up her job as Céleste had said she did, after saying that? Something must have happened during the few days she had been away from the store and she must find out what it was. Because if, as she suspected, Mollie had been dismissed without notice, then she must do something quickly to put matters right for her.

Barely half an hour after she had made that decision Sara was knocking on the door of the terrace house in which Mollie had lived all her life. It was Mollie herself who opened the door to her.

'Sara!' she exclaimed with pleasure. 'I'm so glad to see you. Come in, won't you?'

'Thanks, Mollie. I've just heard you'd gone and I must know the truth. Did you walk out of your job?'

Mollie smiled wryly and shook her head.

'No, I didn't. I was sacked without notice.'

'Then it was my fault,' Sara said in distress.

'It doesn't matter whose fault it was now, Sara, because I'm not sorry it happened.'

'But you told me you couldn't afford to lose your job.'

'No more I can, but it was really a blessing in disguise. You'll never believe this, Sara, but after Céleste sacked me when I came in that morning. I walked about a bit wondering what to do and ran right into Ralph Martin. Do you remember him?'

'Dad's confidential clerk? Yes, of course.'

'Well, he's Personnel Manager at Jones's, the big store in the centre of town. When I told him what had happened he offered me a job right away. It seems they'd been looking for an older, reliable person for a while. I start next Monday. Isn't that great?'

'It certainly is,' Sara answered with relief. 'I'm glad for you, Mollie, though I'm going to miss you. You were the last of the old staff who knew Dad.'

She sighed, and Mollie said quickly,

'Don't worry so much, Sara. Things will come right for you, I'm sure they will.'

'I wish I was as sure. Can I talk to you about something very confidential, and will you promise you won't speak about it to anyone? Anyone at all.'

'You know you can, and that I won't tell a soul.'

Sara told her the story Terry had brought back from France with him, and Mollie's reaction was all she had hoped for.

'It's nothing but a pack of lies,' she said scornfully. 'Fancy expecting us to believe that Mr David was living a double life for sixteen years and none of us guessed! It's ridiculous. Anyway, he wasn't the type, not Mr David.'

Sara breathed a sigh of relief.

'That's what I felt, too, only the evidence Terry talked about seemed so conclusive, I began to have doubts. But now you've helped to clear them away again.'

'What are you going to do?'

'I'll go to Paris and see this woman, then try and check if the marriage really took place. If only my French was a bit better! It's going to be murder trying to communicate with everyone.'

'You'll manage, I'm sure, and I'll be glad to know how you get on. Will you come and have a cup of tea with Mother? She often talks about you and she'll love to see you. You needn't be afraid. Her mind's razor sharp still, but she can't get about as she used to,' she added, seeing Sara's momentary hesitation.

'That's not what's worrying me. I was wondering if I'd have time, that's all. I've got to see Terry again to get this woman's address, then make plane bookings—'

'There's time enough for that. A sit down and a cup of tea will do you good. Come along now.'

When Sara finally left Mollie's home she had to admit that she had been right. The quiet interlude spent talking to Mrs Ingham about the old times had had a calming effect on her and had helped to put the news Terry had given her into its proper perspective.

She was quite sure now of what she must do in order to prove David's innocence of the charge Terry had brought against him. Though how she was going to do it was, she knew, a different matter.

For the first time she regretted that she had not taken more interest in the French lessons she had had at school. Then perhaps she would have been able to talk intelligently to this Frenchwoman and understand what she was saying. Though she was determined not to allow that difficulty to stand in the way of her finding out the truth.

She pushed open the door of her office and walked in, then stopped, feeling the hot colour rush into her cheeks, as Brent Maxwell turned from his contemplation of the yard which was all that could be seen from the window and said,

' Hello, Sara. I hope you don't mind me coming in to wait. White said you wouldn't be long and as you'd left the books open on your desk, I thought he was probably correct.'

She sat down, the annoyance she had felt at her reaction to his presence hardening at his words into an anger which was deflected from herself to him at the implied reproof in them.

' They're all right! I don't expect people to walk in and out of my office examining everything on the desk. Anyway, there aren't many who could interpret them properly,' she said defensively.

' I wasn't criticising you, Sara. I'm sure you're very careful. I'm sorry if you're annoyed because I came in to wait.'

She moved impatiently.

' Of course I'm not annoyed. What did you

come for?'

'Just to ask how you're geting on. Have you talked to Mollie again about the missing stock?'

'No. She isn't here any longer.' Briefly she told him what had happened. 'I've just been to see her. That's where I was when you came. Thank goodness she's found another job. I'd have felt very guilty if she hadn't, because it's all my fault for telling Terry what she said.'

He frowned.

'You think that's why she was dismissed?'

'Yes, definitely.'

'And she's got another job?'

'Yes. Isn't that lucky? What a relief!'

'It must be, so why are you looking so bothered, Sara?'

She was taken aback by his words, thinking how little those deep-set eyes of his missed, suddenly wanting to tell him what had happened, to ask for his advice and help. Yet how could she? He had done so much for her, for them. It was hardly fair to expect him to come to her aid once again.

'What's troubling you, Sara? Won't you tell me?' he asked, so kindly that all her defences disintegrated in a moment.

'I don't see why you should be bothered with my worries, Brent. It isn't fair.'

'Let me be the judge of that. What is it, Sara?'

She leaned back wearily in her chair, and

brushed her hands over her face, closing her eyes so that she did not see him take a step towards her, his hand stretched out. By the time she looked up again, he was sitting on the edge of the desk, looking gravely at her, and she began hesitantly to tell him the story Terry had brought back from Paris.

He listened without interruption until she said at last,

'I can't accept that without seeing this woman myself, and her children, too. But if she doesn't speak any English, I know it'll be hopeless. I'll never be able to understand what she's saying.'

'You feel this is something she and Terry have cooked up between them?'

'I don't know. I only know it can't be true,' she replied helplessly.

'Why should he do that?'

'Because it changes the whole situation. You see, I won't sell because of Val and Jamie, but if this woman's eldest son is the heir, then selling's the best thing for them.'

He frowned.

'Why is that?'

'Because she says she'll give them part of the proceeds.'

He looked at her compassionately.

'Did you know your brother very well?'

'I thought I did. Oh, I know he was years and

years older than me, but he was always very good to me, Brent, and to other people as well. He'd never have treated Val and Jamie like this. Mollie agrees with me. It's completely out of character.'

'And you intend to prove you're right?'

'Yes. I want to see these proofs she says she has and follow them up—'

She stopped, realising suddenly the magnitude of the task she had set herself, and he said quickly,

'Would you like me to come with you?'

Her face lit up with relief.

'Would you? Oh, I'd be so glad!' Then the light died away again. 'But I can't expect you to drop everything and go to France with me. It may take weeks to get at the real truth.'

'That's my problem, isn't it? And unlike you, Sara, I speak French fluently. I have to in my job. You'll be much more likely to get to the bottom of things quickly if I'm there to interpret for you.'

'I know that. It's just—I know I shouldn't take advantage of your generosity, Brent, but I'm going to. Thank you for offering. I—'

'There's no need to thank me,' he interrupted. 'I'm as keen as you are to find out what's been going on. Don't forget I've got a vested interest in the outcome.'

Some of the pleasure she had felt in his offer of help died away at his words and she knew a deep sense of disappointment. She had thought he was doing this solely to help her, though why she should have done she did not know, when she had been nothing but a nuisance and a hindrance to him right from the first moment they had met.

At least, she told herself sadly, he was honest about it and did not pretend to an interest which he did not feel. And, whatever his reasons, he had solved her most pressing problem of how to communicate intelligently with the woman who claimed to be David's legal wife.

But even that knowledge did not lessen the depression which hung over her like a dark cloud.

CHAPTER XI

When Brent had gone to make the arrangements for their journey to France, Sara soon followed him to go and see Terry. He was not in his office and she found him after a while in the salon with Céleste. As she walked towards them they stopped talking and turned to look at her, waiting in silence for her to reach them.

'I'm sorry to interrupt, Terry, but I must talk to you.'

'That's all right, Sara. What is it?'

Sara waited for a moment, then as Céleste did not move, she said pointedly,

'I'd like to speak to Mr White privately, Céleste.'

She did not answer, but turned on her heel and walked away, her back rigid with anger.

Terry frowned.

'Was that necessary, Sara? You've offended Céleste.'

'I'm sorry, but I didn't want her to hear what I've got to say.'

'Why ever not? I've no secrets from her.'

'Maybe you haven't, but I don't want her here when I talk about David.'

'I don't think there's anything else to be said,

Sara.'

'Oh, but there is. I want that woman's address, Terry, so that I can go and talk to her.'

He frowned, his face suddenly becoming sharp and his eyes wary,

'What good will that do you? Unless of course you're a good French linguist. Are you?'

'No, I'm not, but——'

'Then what's the point in going all that way? I've seen all the papers she has and I'm convinced she's telling the truth.'

'Well, I'm not,' Sara said definitely, 'and I've got to be before I accept what you've told me. Surely you can understand that, Terry?'

He made a sudden movement and she stepped back, thinking for a second that he was about to strike her. Then he controlled himself with an obvious effort and his mouth twisted into a smile.

'I do, of course, my dear. This must have been a real blow to your plans. All I'm afraid of is that you'll be wasting your time and your money. I don't think Yvonne Blake will want to see you.'

'Why not?'

'Well, apparently David told her you and your father were bitterly opposed to his marriage and refused to see either her or the children. That's why she didn't get in touch when David died. Why she wrote to me instead.'

'But that's ridiculous!'

He shrugged.

'But understandable. So you see, there's no point in going all that way.'

She did not reply, but stood frowning into space, trying to assess this new information. On the face of it, it seemed reasonable enough, yet there was something in the way Terry had looked at her out of the corners of his eyes, in a faint nuance in his voice, which made her doubt the truth of what he said.

'That's a risk I must take,' she said at last. 'If she won't see me, then I'll have to find some other way. Employ a lawyer or something like that. But I've got to go, Terry.'

His lips thinned angrily.

'Are you being deliberately insulting, Sara?'

'Of course not. What do you mean?'

'I don't like being called a liar any more than the next man,' he said sharply.

'I'm sorry if you think that,' she said wearily. 'It's just that I've got to be sure. Otherwise I'll have to ignore this woman's claim and carry on as I've been doing.'

'You mean you'd still refuse to sell? Even though Yvonne wants money for herself and your brother's children?'

'I've got to be convinced first that they are David's children, and she's got to convince me herself,' she said steadily.

He gnawed at his lower lip, his face a picture of indecision.

'In that case, there's nothing else to be done. I'll write the address out for you and an introduction telling Yvonne who you are and asking her to see you as a favour to me.'

'Thank you. Can I have it today, because I want to go over as soon as travelling arrangements can be made.'

'Very well.' He looked at her cautiously. 'You say you don't speak French? Then perhaps I'd better go with you to interpret, otherwise you'll get nowhere fast.'

'Thank you, but Brent Maxwell is coming with me,' she said, knowing that under no circumstances would she have allowed Terry to accompany her and glad that she could refuse his help so easily.

She saw an angry glitter in his eyes and it seemed as if she was looking at a complete stranger, a stranger who made her feel very afraid.

Then, as quickly as it had come, the impression was gone and he was smiling at her again in his usual charming way, his voice rueful as he said quietly,

'I'm sorry you don't trust me, Sara. It hurts to know that you'd rather go to a complete stranger for help than to me whom you've known for so long. But I suppose I can't expect anything else. You've been away from us all too long.'

Against her will she felt guilty, which was completely irrational but nonetheless very real, and she heard herself apologising in what she realised was a very weak way.

'Then won't you change your plans and let me come with you instead?' he asked persuasively.

Sara shook her head.

'I can't do that. Brent's already making the plane bookings for us both. I'm sorry, Terry.'

'I know just how much that means,' he said sharply. 'You can keep your apologies. I know their real value.'

He turned angrily and she called after his retreating back, 'Don't forget to let me have the address,' but as she went back to her office was still not sure whether he would now implement his promise. And if he did not, how could she force him to?

But she need not have worried. Perhaps the threat to ignore the Frenchwoman's claim had been enough to make him do as she wished. Whatever the reason, before the store closed that night an envelope was brought to her with the address on the outside and apparently the promised letter of introduction within.

She sat with it in her hand for a long time, looking down at the name, thinking how strange and alien it looked, and for the first time wondered how she was going to explain her unexpected trip to

Paris to Val.

All the way home she worried over that problem, but she need not have done. As soon as she knew who was accompanying Sara she asked no further questions.

'You're so lucky,' she said enviously. 'I wish I could come too, but he wouldn't want me. I used to ask David to take me with him sometimes, but he never would. There was always some excuse why I couldn't go.'

Sara's heart sank at those words because perhaps they could mean that Terry was right. There seemed no other reason why now and again David should not have taken his wife with him to Paris, unless it was because he already had another wife and family there.

But she still could not believe it was true. The real answer must be that he had gone to work, and having Val with him would have meant that no work could be done, because she would insist on him accompanying her wherever she wanted to go.

She got up and moved around her bedroom restlessly, wishing she knew the truth and wondering whether or not Brent had been able to make the plane bookings. Because she did not think she could have borne another day of this suspense if he had not.

When the telephone rang at last she was almost

afraid to answer it, yet was relieved to hear Brent's decisive voice.

'Sara? I've booked seats on the plane leaving mid-morning tomorrow. I'll call for you at eight o'clock. Be ready.'

'Oh, good! Thank you, Brent. Will you have breakfast here?'

'All right, you'd better make it seven-thirty, then. You've got the address?'

'Yes, and a letter to this woman.'

'What does it say?'

'I don't know. The envelope's sealed.'

He was silent for a while, then said abruptly,

'I think you should open it.'

'I can't do that.'

'Why not?'

'It isn't addressed to me.'

She heard the amusement in his voice, although all he said was, 'All right, I'll see you in the morning, then. Goodbye, Sara.'

She put the receiver down, feeling all the old annoyance returning. She was foolish to have worried. Brent Maxwell never failed. She might have known he would get exactly the seats he wanted, just as she should have expected him to be as autocratic and dictatorial as he had been.

Only she had not, perhaps because he had been so kind and sympathetic to her earlier.

'Who was that?' Val asked, interrupting her

147

disturbed thoughts.

'Brent Maxwell. He's booked the plane seats and we're—'

'I don't know how you do it, Sara!' Val shook her head. 'First your Johnnie in America and now Brent Maxwell. But perhaps Brent doesn't know about Johnnie, so he won't be jealous.'

'Don't talk nonsense, Val. There's no question of that,' Sara answered shortly, and went into her room before Val could say anything else.

She sat down on the bed, wondering why she should suddenly feel so depressed. Perhaps it was because Val had reminded her that apart from cabling Johnnie her new address and telephone number, she had not thought about him for days, this man whom she had hated to leave to come back to England.

She was quite ready when Brent came next morning. They ate breakfast in the little dining alcove off the kitchen and did not talk much until they had eaten. Then he leaned back in his chair and said,

'Have you decided what you're going to say to this woman?'

'No. I thought I'd wait until she comes—'

'I see.' Thoughtfully he stirred his coffee and for the first time since she had known him, Sara studied his face.

Why had she never noticed before how strong and steadfast he looked, how kind the curve of his mobile lips was?

He looked up and held her gaze with his without speaking, and she felt the blood begin to pound through her veins and was quite incapable of turning away from him, almost mesmerised by him.

Then he smiled, his whole face lighting up.

'We'd better go, Sara, if we're to be at the airport in good time,' he said.

She got up quickly, still feeling disturbed and shaken.

'Yes. I won't be a moment.'

She hurried out of the kitchen, glad of the opportunity to be alone, to try to control the hurried beat of her heart. By the time she came back she had regained control of herself and was able to meet him quite calmly.

He took her case from her and carried it to his car. Soon they were on their way, starting what she knew could be a fateful journey with this man who so short a time before she had not even known, but on whom she was relying without any doubt that he would do everything he could to help her.

It was not until they were on the plane and airborne that he asked her for the letter Terry had given her. She handed it to him and he looked at it frowningly, turning it over in his strong, shapely hands.

149

'Did he tell you what he was going to write, Sara?'

'Yes. He said it was an introduction to me, telling her who I am and asking her to let me see all the papers she had shown to him.'

'It's odd he bothered to seal it if that's all it says.'

'You think there's more in it than that?'

'Could be. I feel we ought to read it.'

She shook her head.

'I wouldn't like to do that—'

He laughed and put his hand over hers, and she was conscious of a thrill like an electric shock which leaped up her arm at his touch. Her hand stiffened under his and at the movement he took his own away quickly.

'You can't have those kind of scruples in a case like this. If this story is really a fabrication cooked up by White to make you sell out, then this letter may contain the proof.'

She did not reply at once, fighting an intense desire to take hold of his hand again, and deriding herself for her stupidity.

'I know I suspected that,' she answered at last, 'but when I really thought about it, I couldn't believe it was true. Terry was anxious for me to accept this offer, but that's a bit different from going to all this trouble to force me to. Why should he? It makes no difference to him who owns the store.'

'That's true, and he'd be more likely to lose his job under new ownership. Take-overs nearly always put executive positions in jeopardy.'

'I suppose so.'

'So there can really only be one explanation. He's the person making the offer.'

She swung round towards him, her eyes wide with amazement.

'Terry is? I don't believe that. Where on earth would he get the money from?'

'A bank or a finance house, perhaps.'

She was silent as she considered that suggestion in the light of her own experience in America, then shook her head decisively.

'He'd never get enough backing, Brent. Oh, I realise the offer wasn't nearly as good as it should have been, but we'd have improved it during negotiation. He must have known that no financier would back an unknown risk, like he is.'

'Then he must have managed to get money from some other source. Any ideas about that?'

Unbidden, there came into her mind the discrepancies she had found in the stocks, the sharp drop in store takings even though the staff said they were busier than they had ever been. All of which had been followed by the dismissal of Mollie, who had confirmed some of her suspicions.

But she did not mention them to Brent, because at that moment the instruction was given to fasten seat belts, and in the bustle of landing there was no opportunity to tell him.

CHAPTER XII

It was not until they were on the way from the airport that Brent mentioned the letter again.

Then he said casually,

'On second thoughts, Sara, I think this letter says exactly what White said it does. It'd be too risky for him to put anything else in it, in case it was opened and read. If he had any instructions for this woman, I imagine he'd have telephoned her today.'

'I think so, too. I'd have hated to open it, Brent. I'd much rather wait until we've got in touch with her, then give it to her intact.'

But when they reached their hotel they found everything taken out of their hands.

'Miss Blake?' the reception clerk said. 'Ah, yes. I have a message for you here.'

He handed her a typewritten card and she took it, slowly translating it before giving it to Brent.

'She's coming this evening? Isn't that what it says?'

'Yes.'

'Before we've contacted her. How would she know where we were?'

'I imagine White must have told her. I always stay here when I come to Paris, and he'd only to ring my office to confirm where we'd be.'

' I see,' Sara said quietly, and for the first time began to feel afraid.

Afraid of meeting this Frenchwoman, of being shown, perhaps, irrefutable proofs. Of having to accept them and go back to England to break the news to Val that she had never been married to David. That Jamie was illegitimate.

Afraid, too, of the heavy responsibility she had assumed.

Because if what Terry had said was true, and the woman was prepared to settle some money on them both, then might not she, by her actions, have jeopardised even this assistance which was being offered to them?

Yet even as she thought it, she knew she had done the only possible thing. That never could she have accepted tamely this terrible accusation against her half-brother.

Those fears were mirrored in her expressive face and Brent looked at her keenly, then put a comforting arm around her.

' What's wrong, Sara?' he asked anxiously. ' Aren't you feeling well?'

She leaned against him gratefully, drawing strength from his nearness, even above her fears aware of him with every part of her body.

' I'm all right.' She drew away from him, pushing back the thick, honey gold hair shakily. ' I

—I suddenly realised that I might have to accept this woman as David's wife, then go back and have to break the news to Val.'

His lips tightened.

'It's damnable that you should be subjected to all this worry. I wish—'

He stopped, and after a moment she said,

'What do you wish?'

'Nothing,' he said brusquely. 'It's too soon for that.'

She looked down, confused by his words. What could he mean by them? Too soon? Too soon for what?

But she knew she would not be given an answer to those questions, because the familiar closed look was back on his face and it was set in the uncompromising lines she had known when she first met him, but which had been absent recently.

'No use crossing that bridge till we come to it,' he said, breaking the silence between them. 'Let's go out and do the town, Sara. Enjoy ourselves and see as much as we can. Shall we?'

She smiled up at him.

'Yes, let's. I've never been to Paris before, so it's all new to me.'

'Good. Then I can take you to all my favourite places. Go and pretty yourself up, my dear, and I'll meet you here in twenty minutes. Not a moment longer, mind.'

'I'll be here,' she said, and crossed to the lift, feeling a surge of happiness which made her want to laugh out loud. Because, she told herself as she washed, then dressed carefully, she was going to be shown Paris, by a man to whom it was familiar and loved.

No wonder she was excited as she applied a light make-up with fingers which trembled with anticipation. Brent was right. She must enjoy this break while she could and forget about the ordeal which faced her when evening came.

He was already in the foyer when she came down. He held out his hand to her and she put hers into it, finding the action quite natural. It seemed to be part of the mood of golden anticipation which filled her.

That was the beginning of a halcyon time, during which she was shown a facet of Brent Maxwell's character which until then she had not known existed. A happy, almost boyish side, when he enjoyed the small things which mean so much.

They were both very gay and lighthearted. They went down into the Metro and found their way to the sugar cake which was the Sacré Coeur, climbing the steps and looking over Paris, spread out below them.

Then they walked around Montmartre, sitting at a table in the Place du Tertre, watching the students and artists, many in strange and wonderful garb. They drank coffee, at the same time imbibing the atmosphere, so different from anything Sara had ever known.

During that day Sara lost her heart to Paris and was blessed with a greater happiness than she had ever experienced before in her twenty-one years.

It was not until they were coming to the end of their evening meal that she came down to earth again, when Brent looked at his watch and said with a sigh,

'Our freedom's nearly over, Sara. We must go back to the hotel. It's almost time for our appointment.'

She stared at him hardly understanding him, the real reason why they had come to Paris so far forgotten that it was like a physical jolt to be reminded of it, and for a moment she felt as if she could not bear to face the woman she had come to see.

Then she pulled herself together and picked up her handbag.

'Is it nearly time?' she asked, and when he nodded, said, 'Then let's go quickly. We mustn't keep her waiting.'

'I'll see about a taxi for us,' he said, and while they waited they were silent and serious for the first time for many hours.

It was as though somebody had drawn a thick curtain, Sara thought, shutting off the golden hours they had spent together, a curtain which would shed gloom and darkness over them for the next few hours. Perhaps for even longer.

In the taxi she twisted her hands together until they were taken in Brent's hard clasp and he held them so until they arrived at the hotel, bringing her warmth and comfort, and a lessening of the tension which had been steadily building up within her.

'I hope she isn't late, Brent.' The breath caught in her throat as they went into the hotel. 'I don't think I can stand the waiting.'

'Yes, you can,' he said, and pulled her closely against him.

She relaxed, gaining strength from his nearness as she had done once before, from the faint male scent of his jacket against her face, and gradually the blood stopped pounding through her head.

She moved away from him and he smiled down at her.

'All right, Sara?'

'Yes, Brent. Thank you.'

They went together to the desk, but before they could ask if there had been a caller for them, the clerk said,

'Mademoiselle Blake? A visitor has come for you. She sits over there.'

Sara turned slowly and looked across to the lone figure dressed in funereal black, sitting very upright in an easy chair.

For a moment her legs refused to move, then she felt Brent's hand under her elbow and heard his voice say authoritatively, 'Come along, Sara,' and went with him to where the woman was waiting for them.

She looked up as they approached and Sara thought she saw a flicker of uneasiness in her narrowed eyes, but when she spoke her voice was firm enough.

'*Bonsoir, mademoiselle, m'sieur.*'

'*Bonsoir.* This is Miss Blake,' Brent said in his fluent French. 'You are the person she's come to meet?'

'*Oui.* I am Madame David Blake.'

'Then let us talk together. Sit here, Sara.' He waited until she had seated herself, then sat down opposite the Frenchwoman and continued, 'Miss Blake wants to see the proofs you have of this marriage with her half-brother. Have you brought them?'

'*Oui,* but first I must see the letter.'

Silently Sara handed it to her and she ripped it open and read it carefully.

'*Merci.*' She unzipped the briefcase which was on a low table beside her and took out some papers. 'Here is the certificate of our marriage, and these are the photographs of our children—David's children,' she emphasised with a challenging look at Sara.

Sara looked helplessly at Brent.

'She's speaking much too quickly for me. I can't make out a word of it. What's she saying?'

He told her briefly, looking with a frown at the Frenchwoman, who sat without expression, as if she was not even remotely interested in what he and Sara were saying. Because even if she could not understand it, there should have been the same look of strain on her face as there had been on Sara's as she had struggled to follow the conversation.

He picked up the marriage certificate and translated it to Sara before putting it down again on the arm of the chair he occupied, then held out his hand for the photographs.

'These are the children?'

'*Oui*. Our three sons. Antoine, Émile and Georges. Are they not like their father? It was he who took them. He was so proud of his boys.'

Brent passed the snaps to Sara.

'Are they like David, do you think?'

She spread them out in front of her, looking at them carefully, seeing three nice-looking boys, very French in appearance, and noticed that the middle one had a vaguely familiar look about him.

'This one—Émile, is it? He reminds me of somebody, but it isn't David. Jamie is like him, very like the snapshots we have of his father at the same age, but these—no!'

'You're sure, Sara?'

160

'Sure? How can I be? If they were in colour —David's hair was so bright, like guinea gold. They all look dark, very dark-haired.' She pointed to the snaps. 'These two are like their mother.'

Brent looked across at the Frenchwoman.

'Have you any colour photographs of the children, *madame*?'

Her eyes narrowed.

'*Non*, I haven't. Only these that I show you.'

'Have you then a picture of yourself and David? On your wedding day perhaps? Or one of him taken with your children?'

'I told you, it was he who took the pictures. Of course he isn't on them. How could he be?'

'*Quel dommage!*' Brent said drily, and Sara looked at him, recognising that phrase easily enough.

'What is a pity? What does she say, Brent?'

He told her and her eyes brightened.

'You think that's important?'

'I think it significant that she shouldn't have any pictures of David. I'd like to keep this certificate and have it vetted.'

He looked at Sara, seeing the strain in her face, and said,

'Would you like something to drink, my dear? And you, *madame*? Can I order you anything?'

'No, I want nothing,' she said sharply. 'Only my rights for my children. That is all.'

S P—F   161

He shrugged.

'Very well. She won't have anything, Sara. What about you?'

'I won't either, Brent. Let's get this over as soon as we can. Please!'

He patted her gently on the arm.

'Relax, Sara. Everything's going to be all right. I'm becoming more and more convinced of it.' He took the certificate in his hand and looked across at the other woman. 'I'd like to borrow this for a day or two, *madame*, if you've no objection.'

She started up from her chair and put out her hand to snatch the paper from him, but he was too quick for her, holding it out of her reach.

'You can't have it,' she panted. 'It's all I have to prove my marriage. Give it back to me!'

He shook his head.

'Not yet. As soon as I've been able to make some enquiries about it, you'll get it back, I promise you.'

'You're a thief! You steal it from me. I'll call the police—'

'Don't be silly,' he said coldly. 'Look, I'll write you a receipt for it.' He watched her with alert blue eyes. 'In any case, even if it is lost you can always get a copy, can't you?'

'That costs money. I've no money for copies.'

'But if your claim holds, you're expecting to have plenty of money?'

'Only for my children, not for myself. Never for myself,' she said quickly.

'Well, there's no need for you to worry. You'll get it back as soon as it can be managed.' He got up and added, 'I think that's as much as we can usefully do now, *madame*. Thank you for coming. It was most kind of you.'

Under his compelling gaze she got up slowly, her face set and sullen.

'And I get nothing for my trouble? Nothing at all?'

'Not until everything is proved to our satisfaction, *madame*. How could it be otherwise?'

She flashed him a look of such hatred that Sara was startled into an exclamation.

'Oh, you English!' she said bitterly. 'Always so smooth. But I will see I get my deserts.'

'You can be sure of that,' he replied with emphasis. '*Bonsoir, madame*.'

For a moment she stood irresolute, then turned and flounced out of the hotel. Brent sat down again beside Sara.

'Well, my dear? What do you think?'

She shook her head.

'I don't know. There's the certificate, and one of the boys looks like somebody I know, but—' She shook her head again. 'What can we do now?'

'I'm going to take this to a lawyer friend of mine and ask him about it.' He frowned. 'You're right

163

about that likeness. I noticed it, too.'

'But it's not David. We should have kept one of those pictures, Brent.'

He laughed.

'We weren't given the opportunity. They were snatched up as soon as we'd looked at them. Suspicious, that. You'd think she'd be glad for you to keep a picture of your nephews, if they are your nephews.'

'That's true.'

'Still, not to worry. We'll get to the bottom of this without them,' he said cheerfully. 'Now I'm going to get you a drink to revive you, then we're going out again for the rest of the evening.'

'Brent, I don't think I could—'

'You're coming out with me whether you want to or not. We'll do a show and then I'll take you to a place I know where we can eat and enjoy ourselves. Now come and have that drink, then away and get changed, ready for our night out.'

She got up, smiling at him mistily.

'All right. I knew you for an autocrat the minute I saw you, Brent Maxwell!'

CHAPTER XIII

It was very late when they returned to the hotel. The night porter was on duty, but Sara hardly noticed him as they walked over to the lift. She was still lapped around by the golden happiness of the hours she had spent with Brent, hours which had filled her with an excitement which pulsed through her like waves of electricity.

He smiled down at her as they waited for the lift to arrive.

'Thank you for a very wonderful evening, Sara,' he said quietly.

'I'm the one who should thank you. Oh, Brent—'

She stopped as the lift doors opened and he put his hand in the crook of her elbow, holding her arm against him as the lift moved silently upwards.

He did not speak, yet Sara was sharply aware of him, in a strange way of his inmost thoughts, as if he was telling her them.

So that when they stopped outside her room door and his hands slid up her arms to her shoulders, it seemed the most natural thing in the world for him to draw her to him.

'Sara,' he said softly, then his arms went around her, holding her gently yet so firmly as he kissed her, lightly at first, then with an increasing passion which brought forth an answering response from her.

When at last he let her go she was aware of him as she had never yet been aware of any man, feeling his heart hammering against her, her own pulses beating in reply.

For a while longer they stood close together, not speaking or moving, then he kissed her again, very gently this time.

'Goodnight, my little love,' he whispered, so quietly that afterwards she could not be sure she had heard him aright. 'If only all my dreams and hopes could come true!'

Then he opened the door for her and she went in, feeling bereft and very much alone as he closed it behind her, aching for him in a way which came as a shock to her, so that she turned quickly and opened the door again, going into the corridor and looking eagerly for him.

But he had gone. Only the long expanse of golden carpet stretched before her, empty and forlorn.

She was still in a bemused state as she got ready for bed, and for a while she lay awake, savouring those blissful moments, until at last she drifted into a deep sleep.

She was awakened in the morning by the chambermaid bringing her breakfast and sat up in bed, responding automatically to her greeting.

' *Un billet, mademoiselle*,' the maid said, indicating the envelope on the tray, and there was all the wisdom of the ages in her smiling glance.

' *Merci bien*,' Sara said, feeling the colour rise to her cheeks, and she did not open the envelope until the chambermaid had gone.

Then she tore it open with suddenly trembling fingers. It was headed 8.30 a.m.

' Sara,' she read, ' I'm going now to see my friend, but will be back in time to take you out to lunch. I'll be in the foyer from 12.30 p.m. Please be ready and waiting. Brent.'

She looked down at the note, aware of a deep stab of disappointment. What she had expected she did not know. Certainly not this cool and casual information about his plans, that read as if it was from a complete stranger. Not after last night.

She felt tears of disappointment sting in her eyes, and fought them back with determination. She might have known how it would be, that the moments which had been so precious to her had been for him merely the satisfaction of a whim.

And in addition to everything else, in his usual high-handed and arrogant way he had calmly taken everything into his own hands without consulting her, without even bothering to find out whether or not she wanted to go with him to see this lawyer.

Then he had finished up by ordering her to be in the foyer to meet him at half past twelve, 'ready and waiting'.

Well, this time, she told herself angrily, he was going to be disappointed, because she had no intention of waiting tamely in the hotel until he decided to come and take her out to lunch. She would lunch by herself and go back to the hotel when and if it suited her.

Quickly she ate her breakfast, then dressed and left the hotel, determined to stay away until she was sure Brent would have become tired of waiting for her and would have gone.

But the shops had no power to interest her and she walked past them and through them unseeingly, hardly able to believe that the time was passing so slowly, able to think of nothing but what Brent was doing, how he was faring in his quest for the truth she was so anxious to discover.

It was a long while before that thought really became meaningful to her, but when it did she stopped, heedless of the people in whose way she was standing, staring at a display of shoes in a nearby shop window with unseeing eyes.

The truth she was so anxious to discover. She said the words over and over again to herself, the anger she had felt against Brent disappearing in her own self-analysis.

The truth which, in such an unselfish way, he

had left his own concerns and travelled with her to France to discover. He was, that morning, without complaint, seeing his friend in order to ask him to examine and find out more about this certificate which seemed to record David's marriage to the Frenchwoman, to whom he had talked with such patience and understanding.

And in addition he had taken her about, had entertained her royally, had shown her the Paris he loved, and had himself been a charming and wonderful companion.

Then in order to reward him for all he had done and was doing, because she was angry with him, because she had thought his note cool and offhand, she intended to leave him waiting for her in the hotel foyer while she deliberately stayed away, to teach him a lesson.

She felt shame surge through her as she acknowledged that it was not Brent who needed to be taught a lesson but herself—a lesson on how to be grateful for the help he had given so freely to her.

She moved then, hurrying back to the hotel against a clock which now seemed to be rushing ahead madly. She saw him as soon as she walked through the doors, sitting in one of the chairs in the foyer, relaxed and handsome.

Sara stood just inside the door, feeling suddenly afraid, fighting the urge to turn and run away in case the news he may have brought would confirm all her worst fears.

Then he looked up and saw her standing there.
He got up and came to her, holding out both hands
and smiling in a way which twisted her heart
within her.

She put her hands into his, feeling confused and
shy, acutely aware of him, of his deep set eyes with
their smiling look.

'Hello, Sara. Come and sit down while I tell
you all I've found out before we go in to lunch.
I ordered a dry sherry for you,' he added as the
waiter put the glasses on the table. 'All right?'

'Yes, thank you,' she said breathlessly. 'Tell me
what your friend said.'

'There's no doubt about it! That certificate
has been forged, Sara.'

'Brent, is it true? Really true? But that's the
most wonderful news!'

'Yes, isn't it? Someone has very carefully
erased the man's signature and substituted David's.'

'You're sure? It seemed—I've been afraid to
acknowledge it even to myself, but it seemed very
like his writing.'

'It may have done, but nevertheless it's a
forgery! I saw it under a microscope and there's
no doubt about it.'

Sara put down the glass she had been holding, her
hands trembling.

'I can't believe it. I didn't notice anything

really wrong with the signature.'

'Neither did I, but then it's obvious we weren't meant to have the chance to examine it properly. That's why Madame was so livid when I refused to give it back to her.'

Sara looked bewildered.

'But why should she do such a thing?'

'Not her,' he answered quietly. 'White.'

'Terry? It doesn't seem possible!'

He leaned forward, clasping his hands together.

'Doesn't it? Think, Sara. Who told you he'd had a good offer for the store but couldn't or wouldn't tell you the name of the intending buyer? Who has always tried to force you to sell, even enlisting Val's help?'

'Terry,' she said slowly.

He nodded.

'Now think again, Sara. You said there was a likeness between one of the boys and somebody you couldn't put a name to. Who was he like? Not David.'

'No, not David, but not Terry either.' She stopped, a frown between her brows as she concentrated on that problem. Then with dawning comprehension she breathed, 'Of course! Céleste! That's who he reminded me of.'

'That's right—Céleste Durand. My lawyer friend checked up and found that the original certificate was of a marriage between Maurice d'Islay and Yvonne Durand.'

'Is she—Céleste's sister, then?'

'Yes.'

Sara was silent, struggling to accept this knowledge and finding it almost impossible to believe. How could Terry, who had known her almost all her life, whom her father and David had trusted, have been so dishonest?

Because she was not misled by Céleste's involvement in the plot. She knew perfectly well that it was Terry who must be behind it.

'It doesn't make sense!' she burst out at last.

He smiled compassionately.

'Yes, it does, Sara. Remember, he's been with Blake's almost all his working life, thirty years or more. Don't you see, he would gradually begin to look on the firm as his own, to identify himself with it.'

'Perhaps he might, only—'

'When your father died he probably expected to take his place. Instead David took over and Terry was still playing second fiddle. When David was killed it must have seemed as if fate was taking a hand. Here was his big chance, if he could buy the business cheaply enough. He thought Val would be in control and had talked her over when you came home and then he discovered just how wrong he was.'

'Yes, I can understand that,' she said slowly.

'But this way of trying to force my hand. This woman, Yvonne Durand, would have had to be paid, and then there was Val. She was going to benefit, too.'

'He would only have had to pay Val, wouldn't he? Yvonne would no doubt have received something for her trouble, but think of the advantages to Terry. You'd have been outvoted and he'd have got the business even more cheaply than he expected to.'

'But why pay Val? Why didn't he try to get away with that as well?'

'Because that was part of the bargain, I imagine.'

She stared at him in disbelief.

'You mean Val was a party to this—this fraud? Oh, no. I don't believe that!'

'Perhaps she didn't actually know the method by which Terry hoped to force your hand, Sara, but I think she must have been aware of the intent, don't you?'

Sara frowned, looking back over the past weeks, remembering the way Val had shrugged off any serious talk about the store while supporting Terry all the time, and though it hurt her to do so, she had to acknowledge that he might be right.

'What shall we do now, Brent?' she asked, all the pain she felt at this tale of duplicity mirrored in her expressive face.

'I think we ought to go back home. I've booked seats on the afternoon plane. Is that all right?'

She nodded.

'And Yvonne?'

'My friend will return the marriage certificate to her and point out the penalty for forgery. We'll wait and see what happens after that.'

'I see. Brent—'

He smiled.

'What's troubling you, Sara?'

'Your friend—he won't do anything to Yvonne? I don't want her and her sons to suffer because of Terry.'

He patted her hand gently.

'He isn't going to do anything except warn her of the consequences if she should be involved in that kind of fraud again.'

She breathed a sigh of relief.

'I'm glad about that. The boys looked so bright and friendly. Such nice boys.'

He laughed then.

'You're much too soft-hearted to be an American business tycoon, Sara, though I'm not saying that's a bad thing.' He got up, then took her hands in his and pulled her to her feet, smiling down at her in a way which made her forget her resolutions about this man. 'Come and have lunch, then afterwards we'll have to pack and get off to the airport.'

He was still holding her hand when they went

into the restaurant and only released it when the waiter showed them to a table for two in one of the long windows.

But all the way through lunch and afterwards, when they were driving to the airport, she could feel that strong, hard clasp, and drew comfort from that memory against the inevitable moment when she would have to face Val and Terry and tell them what she had found out.

He gnawed at his lower lip, his face a picture of indecision.

CHAPTER XIV

It was early evening when the plane landed and they got into Brent's car which he had left at the airport on the way to Paris. Sara felt weary and travel-stained, as though she had been travelling for days instead of only hours, when they finally arrived at the flat.

'Will you come in with me?' she asked Brent, looking at him with pleading eyes. 'It's going to be awful meeting Val, and not letting her see that I suspect—'

'Of course, Sara,' he said at once. 'Don't worry so much. It'll be all right, I'm sure. Are you going to tell her why you went to Paris tonight?'

'Yes. I want to get it over with. I don't think I could stand the suspense if I didn't.'

'Are you sure that's the best thing to do? Wouldn't it be better to wait until after we've spoken to Terry tomorrow?'

'No, I'd rather tell Val first. I think it'll be easier that way. I don't want to quarrel with her, Brent, and this way I'll see I don't.'

'Just as you like,' he said, but in the end all her good intentions were wasted.

Because when they walked into the flat the first person she saw was a tall, fair-haired man whom she had thought was in America, but who now bounced out of an easy chair and held out his arms to her.

'Sara, honey! At last! Where've you been? I thought you were never coming.'

'Johnnie!' Her face lit up in happy surprise and she ran to him, feeling his arms close round her in a bearlike hug. 'Where did you spring from?'

He laughed down at her, his hair lying thickly and untidily on his forehead as always.

'I had a couple of days to spare, so I thought I'd better take a flip over and look you up. Say, what are you doing, honey? When are you coming back to me? It's murder at the office without you.'

'Soon now, Johnnie, I hope.' She became aware of Brent standing silently in the doorway and turned towards him. 'I'm sorry, Brent, but I never expected to find Johnnie here. He's my boss in America. This is Brent Maxwell, Johnnie, who has helped me so much since I came home.'

Johnnie held out his hand.

'I certainly appreciate that,' he said. 'I know Sara always thinks she can do everything for herself and I'm not daring to say she's wrong, but it's great she found someone to help her, just the same.'

'Johnnie Acton! I thought you were my friend! Brent will be thinking the very worst about me after that!'

Brent looked at her, his eyes crinkling into a

smile.

'Nothing anyone says will ever alter what I think of you, Sara,' he said. 'I was glad to do what I could to help.'

'That's the idea!' Johnnie put his arm around Sara's shoulders and hugged her to him. 'He's a man after my own heart, honey!'

'Well, Sara, I'd better go. You won't want to talk business now your friend has come over to see you.'

Sara pulled away from Johnnie's arm, feeling suddenly anxious, seeing the old closed expression back again on Brent's face.

'But you'll come tomorrow? I'll have to see Terry, and you did say you'd come with me.'

'If you still want me to.'

'Of course I do. You must know that. You will come?'

He nodded.

'Very well.'

'At ten o'clock as we arranged?'

'Yes. Shall I meet you at the store?'

'No, call for me here. You said you would—'

'But things are a bit different now,' he replied enigmatically. 'However, just as you wish. I'll see you then, Sara.'

He turned to go, but she stopped him, putting her hand urgently on his arm.

'You're sure you won't stay?'

'Yes, why not do that?' Johnnie broke in. 'Val
—Mrs Blake, I mean—she's got a meal nearly ready
for us. I know that because I've been helping with
it. It'll stretch to one more.'

Brent shook his head.

'No, thanks. I've a pile of work waiting for me
and I ought to go and do some of it. Good-night,
Acton. See you tomorrow, Sara.'

He moved towards the door and after a moment's
hesitation Sara followed him.

'I'll see you out, Brent,' she said, and added shyly
as he opened the front door, ' I'm sorry our journey
had to end like this. I wanted to talk to Val tonight
before we saw Terry, but now we can't.'

'Of course not. I wouldn't expect you to when
your friend's arrived to visit you,' he said coldly.
'You'll have other things to think about and talk
about now. Much pleasanter things, that's for
sure.'

'Yes. Yes, I suppose so,' she answered, and
watched until he left the house, before going back
into the flat.

She stood in the hall for a few minutes, trying to
fight the depression which filled her and which she
could not understand. Because surely she should
be on top of the world, now. To come home to
find Johnnie there, to see him again after the past
few weeks of strain, with his infectious grin and
pleasant drawling voice. Not so long ago that

would have been all she wanted. Yet now it had happened she felt none of the excitement and relief it should have brought her.

When she went back into the sitting room Johnnie said,

'So that's the Maxwell fellow! Val was telling me about him. Queer fish, isn't he? Not very friendly.'

'You're quite wrong!' Sara flared up in defence of him quickly. 'He's quite the opposite. No one could have been a better friend to me.'

He shrugged.

'Maybe you're right, hon, but—'

'I am,' she interrupted earnestly. 'He's not easy to get to know, Johnnie, but when you do I'm sure you'll like him.'

'I'm not likely to stay long enough to find out. I've got to fly back the day after tomorrow. I only came to find out what's been happening to you, Sara. Why you hadn't come back as you promised.'

She looked at him guiltily.

'I'm sorry, I ought to have written to you, but there's been so much happening, so many things to do—'

'Don't think about it, honey. Now I've seen you I know the answers.'

She frowned, puzzled by his words, but before she could ask him what he meant Val came in, stopping in the doorway when she saw Sara there, her expression changing.

'You're back! I didn't hear you come in.'

'She came with that Maxwell fellow,' Johnnie said easily, 'but he's gone off now. What about supper, Val? Is it nearly ready? Sara and I are starving, aren't we, honey?'

'Yes. Thirsty, too.'

'Everything's ready.' Val burst into rapid speech. 'Wasn't it wonderful Johnnie turning up like this? We've had quite a day together and he's been helping me with the meal. He's certainly well trained. He can do anything in the kitchen.'

'That's no thanks to me,' Sara laughed. 'It must be his mother's training.'

'You're babbling, Val, honey.' He put an arm around each of them and hustled them through to the kitchen where the table was already spread in the dining alcove. 'Let's eat, before we all fall by the wayside.'

'I'll serve,' Sara said, 'as my contribution to this feast.'

'You'll do no such thing. You'll both sit down and be waited on. Though I'll probably allow you to wash up afterwards. Now, Sara, tell me all about this spot of bother that's kept you from coming back to me.'

Afterwards Sara was to look back on the next two hours and try to sort out her impressions, but without a great deal of success.

She was aware of Johnnie and Val, on the best of terms with each other, laughing and talking together, but she felt too tired, both physically and emotionally, to do more than to try to eat the meal provided for her, and took only a minor part in the chatter between the other two.

She was glad when she could admit to being worn out and could go to her own room and be quiet and alone. The sudden and unheralded appearance of Johnnie, dear as he was to her, after the strain of the last few days, had exhausted her, and the thought of the difficult task which had to be done next day seemed only bearable because Brent had promised to go with her and support her.

Before then she would have to decide how she was going to tackle this interview with Terry, yet as she got into bed, hearing vaguely the others still talking together in the sitting room, she was not thinking of or planning for the morrow.

Instead she was remembering that although Brent had said he would go with her to see Terry in his usual kind way, he had left her quickly, apparently without wanting to stay although he had been pressed to, and with that cold, closed look back on his face again. And she felt deeply worried and hurt. He had been such a wonderful companion when they had been in France, so that even while the fear of discovering that the Frenchwoman's claim had been good had hung over her, she had been happy.

She had thought that at last Brent had come to accept her as a friend and not as a nuisance whose problems he had to solve whether he wanted to or not. The knowledge that she had been wrong made her feel miserable and sick at heart, so that even the coming of Johnnie all the way from America to see her did not raise her spirits.

She turned over restlessly, closing her eyes and trying to woo the sleep which would not come. Instead she saw as though on a film a picture of Brent Maxwell as she had slowly come to know him since their first meeting. As she had learned to love him in spite of herself. Honestly now she acknowledged that without reservation, without denying that truth any longer.

She could feel again his lips on hers as he had kissed her that night in the hotel, and knew now why he had disturbed her so deeply when a kiss from Johnnie had merely been something which gave her surface enjoyment. Poor Johnnie, who had come such a long way to see her. She knew now that she would never marry him, no matter what happened in the future.

Not that she had ever said she would. When he had asked her she had always said, 'Not yet, Johnnie. I'm not ready to get married yet,' and he had always accepted her refusal without any obvious signs of despair. And now she, who had been able to give herself no good reason for refusing him when she was so fond of him, knew that she had been waiting for a deeper feeling, for the love which sacrifices everything for the loved one, a love which follows the loved one to the end of the earth without complaint.

Well, she had found it. She had fallen in love with a man who saw her only as a person whom he had to help, against his will. And although he had done so with the kindness and thoughtfulness which were so much a part of him, she was not deceived.

During that night as she lay sleepless she faced up to the knowledge that the years which stretched before her might be barren and loveless. Because she knew herself too well. For her there could never be a second best. If Brent did not want her, then no one else would do. Not Johnnie, not anyone. But she also made her mind up to accept what she was given and make the most of it, while she could. Then perhaps in the lonely years when she no longer had Brent with her, she might have some happy memories to look back on.

She was ready waiting for him when he came at ten o'clock as he had promised.

'Are you sure you want to see White this morning, Sara?' he asked when he came in. 'Wouldn't you rather wait until Acton goes back so that you can be with him?'

She shook her head.

'No, I'd rather get it over. Anyway, it's too late. He and Val have gone off for the day already,' she said, her voice after the sleepless night and because of the difficult interview before her sounding flat and despondent even to her own ears.

He looked at her with concern.

'You should have gone with them. You could easily have telephoned me. I would have seen White for you.'

'As if I'd let you do that! You've done enough for me, Brent, over the past few weeks, and though I may have seemed ungrateful, I'm not.'

'I don't want thanks from you,' he said briefly.

'Perhaps not, but even though I've taken so much advantage of your kindness, I'm not really the kind of ungrateful type who would push off all my responsibilities on you.'

He took a step towards her.

'I know that, Sara. I think you're—oh, what's the use? When are you going back to America?'

She was surprised by the sudden change of subject and did not know how to reply. She knew very well what was the truthful answer. That she did not want to go anywhere that was not near to him, but she could not tell him that. Once she might have done, when he was the eager and wonderful companion who had made her stay in France so magical. Not now, when he appeared to have forgotten those happy hours.

'We'd better go,' she said abruptly, and walked past him through the door.

He put out his hand as if to stop her, then let it drop back to his side and followed her out of the house to his car.

They did not speak as he drove to the store nor as they walked from the car park and went through the store towards the escalator. But before they reached it they were stopped by the floor manager in a state of great agitation.

'Miss Blake! Thank goodness you've come! I've been trying to contact you all morning, but there was no reply from your home.'

'But I've been in—' Sara began, then recollected the recent move and knew she ought to have let the telephone operator have the new telephone number. 'I'm very sorry, Mr Lewis. We moved house a few days ago. What's happened? Has anything gone wrong?'

'It's Mr White. He hasn't been in this morning and his secretary says his office has been completely cleared out. And Céleste hasn't come in either.'

She looked quickly at Brent, seeing the same look of awareness in his eyes as she knew was in her own.

'Don't worry,' she said quickly. 'We'll probably hear something from them during the day. In the meantime, carry on as usual. I know I can rely on you.'

'Of course you can, Miss Blake,' he said in gratified tones, and she moved across to the escalator with Brent. They did not comment on the new situation until they were standing in Terry's office and had pulled open some of the drawers in the big desk, finding them empty as the manager had said.

'So we're too late,' she said at last, aware of a surge of relief at the words. 'He must have found out that we know and he and Céleste have gone before we could tackle them about it.'

'Yes. I'm sorry, Sara. That must be my fault. I should have told my friend not to send the papers and the warning to Yvonne until today. She must have got in touch with him as soon as she received them. I've made a real botch of it, haven't I?'

She took an impulsive step towards him.

'You can say that after all you've done for me? I'd have got nowhere at all if you hadn't come to Paris with me. I'm glad it's happened this way, Brent. Really glad.'

'Even though they've probably been defrauding you, Sara? Making away systematically with the firm's money?'

She nodded.

'That makes no difference, not as far as Terry's concerned. You see, I've known him practically all my life. When I was a small girl I used to come in here to see my father and Terry was always so

187

kind to me. In those days I hero-worshipped him.
I thought there was nobody like him. I'm glad
he's gone. Dad would have been too, I'm sure of
that.'

'Then I'm glad too,' he said simply. 'Sara—'

He stopped, looking at her silently, and after a
moment she asked,

'Yes, Brent? What is it?'

He went closer to her and put out his hand, and
without hesitation she put hers into it.

'Sara, I want to ask you something. Will you
promise to answer it truthfully, no matter what
that answer may be?'

Her eyes widened and she could feel the blood
begin to throb through her as his hand tightened
on hers, willing herself not to let him see how much
his touch disturbed her.

'I promise,' she said breathlessly.

'I know I've no right to ask you this, Sara, but
I've got to know the answer. Are you in love with
Johnnie? Are you going back to the States to
marry him?'

She did not reply, but stood looking at him,
trying to read in his eyes the reason behind those
questions.

'Sara!' he said urgently. 'You must answer me.
Please!'

'First tell me—why do you want to know?' she
asked softly.

'Because until I do I won't have a minute's peace of mind.'

She felt a surge of happiness thrill through her at his words and saw his face alight with emotion and desire, and swayed towards him, her eyes bright with love and hope.

'No, Brent, I'm not in love with Johnnie, I know that now, and I'm not going back to the States with him.'

His hands moved up her arms and she felt their clasp, warm and urgent, through the coat she was wearing.

'Does that mean I've got a chance, Sara? You must have realised long ago how much I love and want you. Have I, Sara? Have I?'

She put her arms around him and turned her lips up to his.

'Yes, I know now, Brent, and that's my answer. Yes, my dearest love. Yes,' she said, and then there was only silence as his mouth came down demandingly on hers.

Have You Missed Any of These
Harlequin Romances?

All books are 60c. Please use the handy order coupon.

DD

Have You Missed Any of These
Harlequin Romances?

All books are 60c. Please use the handy order coupon.

EE